Bonnie loves drums, music and women. She believes that one day she'll play in the perfect band and have the ideal girlfriend. For a while it seems possible, but ten years ago, the music industry didn't embrace dykes with short hair and Bonnie has to negotiate half-open closets, prying gossip writers, and a broken heart before she can learn the real art of playing. *Timing the Heart* is a story about lesbian sex, growing up, living with your girlfriend's children and finding a sound engineer with principles.

Gina Schien spent babyhood in a migrant hostel and childhood in Maroubra where she developed a love of sand, surf and coconut oil. Living in east Sydney for the last ten years has developed her attachment to flat white, Oxford Street and a view of the harbour. She has worked as a journalist, television producer and editor — her short fiction has been published in magazines, journals and several Australian anthologies.

Also from BlackWattle Press

Novels —
and that's final — Dean Kiley
Wisdom — Rae Desmond Jones
Shadows on the Dance Floor — Gary Dunne
Mayakovsky in Bondi — Sasha Soldatow
Short Fiction —
Fruit — Gary Dunne, Editor
Falling For Grace — Roberta Snow & Jill Taylor, Editors
Angel Tails — Tim Herbert
Poetry —
Flight of Koalas — Margaret Bradstock
The Times of Zenia Gold — Chris Jones
History —
Camping by a Billabong — Robert French
Cartoons —
Living With Adam — Jeff Allan
Biography/Fiction —
Beyond Blood — Louise Wakeling & Margaret Bradstock, Editors

Send SASE for a catalogue, PO Box 4, Leichhardt NSW 2040

Timing
the Heart

GINA SCHIEN

BlackWattle Press
Sydney Australia
1995

Publication of this title was
assisted by the Australia Council,
the Federal Government's arts
funding and advisory body.

Published by BlackWattle Press Pty Ltd
PO Box 4, Leichhardt, NSW Australia 2040
September 1995

© Cover photo Mazz Images 1995
Printed by Australian Print Group, Epping NSW

ISBN 1 875243 20 8

With love for Stacey
who gave me immeasurable support

1

On the day it happened, Bonnie was seventeen and Miss Driver was twenty seven. It was an afternoon when the sea breeze covered the school with a fine layer of salt that powdered the skin and frosted the flag pole that always rattled like plates. Miss Driver was reading a poem with only one or two glances at the page, repositioning the book over her heart as if the poem were an oath she was swearing.

"The winter evening settles down
With smells of steak in passageways.
Six o'clock."

She stopped as if the school buzzer was cued to chime the hour. Someone coughed. There was the squeak and scrape of tennis shoes.

"The burnt out ends of smoky days
And now a gusty shower wraps
The grimy scraps
of withered leaves"

Miss Driver looked directly at Bonnie

"about your feet."

Bonnie suddenly noticed how noble her teacher's face was in the light of the poem and slant of afternoon sun, and strong in the way misunderstood teachers were strong. Miss Driver looked at each of the girls as if to hunt down the one person who might say 'Oh my God. That was beautiful! It was just … ' Bonnie saw the black court shoes and the frayed cuffs of her teacher's pinstriped trousers and nearly leapt to her feet to be that person.

She sat in her small bedroom that night and hunted for the hidden meaning in withered leaves. Or was it grimy scraps? She scanned each line of *Preludes*. People had scribbled notes across the poem, things like: "TS Eliot backwards spells toilETS". Bonnie put the book down. Miss Driver had snuck into her body and was pulsing through her bloodstream like a new virus.

Love bulleted around Bonnie's ribcage and mushed her loins. She held her marked English essays against her face and breathed in their pages for the scent of skin or the print of a thumb. In her quiet room, while surf boomed down at the bay, she scanned the red ink in the tidal margins for signs of her teacher's psyche.

"What exactly are you saying here?" Miss Driver had written on page two. And on page three after one of Bonnie's noble, thundering generalisations: "source?". Each night she ploughed quickly through the square and curly brackets of maths formulae so that she could move on to English and darken page after page with anxious and perfect writing.

Music released itself in an embroidered stream from her record player. She worked on an English essay with relish but was distracted by the music. "Small incongruities and ironies, action juxtaposed next to thought, are touches that ... " Her pen stopped, drifted, sank down to the desk. She wondered, was the music absorbed into the page? Micro sound dots infiltrating wood chip and bleach. Were the lyrics influencing the arguments in her essay?

The singers she liked were usually tormented and thin and they wore black clothes. TS Eliot and Virginia Woolf would have written great lyrics, being tormented in a genteel cardigan-ish way. They would have appreciated music's invisible waves, like pleats in an air landscape.

Bonnie lay on her bed so that the music covered her like a sheet, but it was the drumming that excited her so much that she had to stand up to hear it properly. She even stopped thinking about Miss Driver. In a studio in another country someone had hit those beats out. A man with a cigarette in his mouth, his face expressionless but passion flowing through his feet and hands. And the passion was squeezed out of the spinning vinyl. What a mad mix of science music was!

She paced her room and listened for the formula. One drum made one sort of noise. Another made another. Simple, but when they crossed and double-crossed, electricity ran through them in a current. She sat down at her desk and beat her right heel on the floor without realising, as though at a hypnotist's command. As though she were asleep. Her cells, still pumped full of Miss Driver, wanted to run her body down to the beach to watch the ocean moving as restlessly as the stuff in her veins.

When the house was quiet and musicless, Bonnie looked out of the window at the road. She was calmer. Now it was a question of fate. "If the next car is a Holden she loves me."

She strained for the soft shuush of cars at midnight on asphalt. She put her lips against the glass until white fog rose and fell in a heart-shaped pulse. Sometimes no car passed for hours and she fell asleep with her cheek against the glass. Moths clapped up and down the glass trying to reach her light.

At the start of Bonnie's final year Miss Driver announced that she was about to make an announcement. The class waited, yawning.

"I think we know each other well enough to be on first name terms."

The class shuffled a bit, blew noses, dropped books. Bonnie waited, not breathing.

"So I want you to call me Nora."

Bonnie sat and considered this gift. Nora, such a straight-backed decent name it was and she knew it now, and could say, hey Nora, whenever she wanted. But she didn't dare. Not yet.

2

She walked home in a state of delicate bliss. It was a fine afternoon in Maroubra, golden light was turning broken bottles into sparkling treasure, the scrub bordering the coast road looked less stunted and the house, when she saw it in front of her, felt at peace. Her mother Clara sat in the dining room playing solitaire.

"Pot of tea just made."

Clara watched her daughter, out of reach, floating and then landing on the very edge of a chair to tell her something.

"Miss Driver wants us to call her Nora."

"Nora. Why Nora?"

Her mother must be having her on.

"It's her first name."

"Oh! Good."

Bonnie's mother was pleased. The two distinctive sounds "Miss Driver" were an incantation that her daughter had cast upon the house. But the single word Nora seemed harmless. Without power.

"Nora's a nice name, I think."

Bonnie's smile widened. N.O.R.A. Roan. Roan colt.

"It is, isn't it?"

She galloped up the stairs and into her room in a frenzy of love. Her mother tilted her head to one side and wondered about the space between the second and fourth row of cards. She had two kings she could put there. A black spade and a red heart. Both had unturned cards behind them. She thought about Bonnie's crushes. Miss Swenson (science), Mrs Chessler (maths), Miss Martinelli (Italian). Her daughter's school results mapped and charted the course of her emotions. She moved the red king and his little card family. Upstairs, Patti Smith was blaring. The bass was practically coming through the ceiling. Her daughter's right heel stomped the floor as though it was sending coded messages.

*

And now things started to change. Miss Driver grew even more matey with her mystified class, which needed reminders to call her Nora. A week before their HSC study break she invited them over to her house for dinner. Bonnie knew exactly where that house was. She had looked up N. Driver in the phone book and traced the x and y co-ordinates of the address in her mother's street directory. Jane Gannon, who was school captain, looked uncertain. She would be thinking about numbers and the inconvenience.

"Are you cooking for all of us?"

"Yep. All of you. Bring over any work you're having trouble with."

The class was silent. Bonnie walked home and sat in front of Clara who

3

was reading *The Vivisector*. She waited for her mother to acknowledge her. Her mother did not. Bonnie pulled the book down. Her mother lifted the book back up.

"Bonnie, please. That's very rude."

"Nora's invited us over for dinner on Friday night."

She whispered it as though a baby were asleep in the next room.

"Has she indeed?" Clara put the book down. "Who's us? You and me?"

"Very funny," Bonnie whispered. "The class. And don't worry, I'll get a lift home with someone." Her mind raced ahead. "I might even stay at Sue's place."

She listened to herself with interest. Her cunning was that of a stranger's – desperate, courageous, and spurred on by something unnameable that promised obscure but desirable rewards.

On Friday the class arrived in a large group outside Miss Driver's house and tapped like mice on her front door. Bonnie stood apart from them and scraped her feet uncomfortably. She wore a white shirt, black denim jeans and ancient riding boots. The other girls rustled in silks and light cottons. Some of them clutched tiny evening purses.

"You could have made a bit more of an effort, Bonnie," Jane Gannon said.

Even her best friend Sue Taylor wore something frilly that seemed to accuse Bonnie of violating a code of decency. There was a subdued silence but then the door opened and Nora stood there, in jeans and a T shirt. She held a wooden spoon in her hand. Bonnie shot a quick leer of triumph to Jane Gannon.

"Don't you all look nice! Come in. Don't stand on ceremony."

They came in, or shuffled in, and stood in the front room. They looked around at the walls as though they had stumbled into a gallery full of strange new art that they might be tested on later. Tins of paint cluttered the corners, resting on torn strips of old sheet. A carpet had been taken up recently. Several girls sneezed and then fiddled with their noses, making fine adjustments.

"Sorry about all the dust. I'm renovating," Nora said. "It's taking ages with just me doing it."

She leaned against the wall. Paint smeared the knees of her jeans as if she had kneeled down to pray in a puddle of it. The girls stood in small guarded clumps in the centre of the room. Bonnie could tell that they were shocked by this bachelorish dishevelment. The place was a mess. Jane swivelled around on high heels, careful not to disturb anything.

And then they somehow acclimatised. They enquired about this and that in the self-consciously polished tones of young adults practising small talk.

"Oh yes? Really?" they squeaked.

A chime tinkled somewhere. Jane Gannon and her best friend Elise had

4

brought white wine and a strange stilted out-to-dinner manner.

"I hope you're cooking white meat, Miss D — Nora," Jane said, "because white wine should be drunk with chicken or fish, they say."

Bonnie had brought a bottle of Blackberry Nip in a brown paper bag. Such an important evening could only be carried off with levity and a lack of breeding. And so she would occupy her own unique ground between Jane and Elise's pretensions and the other girls' predictable silence. She stomped straight through the front room and lounge room and into the kitchen, forcing Nora and the girls to follow her. A pot bubbled on the stove. She lifted its lid and sniffed deeply.

"Smells good!" she said.

Nora smiled wryly.

"And that's just the rice," she said.

The class went out into the garden to look at bags of potting soil, freshly delivered piles of manure and a newly planted tree fern. They were arranged in the lounge room on a semi-circle of chairs. They accepted that hot plates of beef curry were to be balanced on their laps.

"Sorry. No table. Yet. No vegetarians I hope?"

"I think we're a bit young for vegetarianism," Jane Gannon said. "We're a bit young to be making those sort of life choices."

Bonnie stared at her, admiring the timetable of her life. She imagined Jane's diary for next year. "June 10 – 12 o'clock, buy new shoes. One o'clock, consider vegetarianism."

A cask of white wine was offered. No-one wanted Bonnie's Blackberry Nip so she kept the bottle next to her on the floor. She dropped her fork, then her knife. The other girls frowned at her. Conversation moved along, lagged and then stopped dead. There was only the sound of girls dealing with rice and meat. Knives scraped china. Bonnie's boots scraped the floorboards.

Did anyone have any school work with them? No-one did. Nora pointed out renovations.

"I've just painted these skirting boards. People told me to do the walls first but I haven't decided on a colour."

People? Bonnie tried to imagine her friends.

"Paint the walls purple, I reckon," she suggested.

The other girls sensed something embarrassing, Bonnie was always good for that, but Nora was interested.

"Why purple?"

"A good feminist colour."

Bonnie looked at Nora and grinned with certain knowledge. She had gone looking for Nora's bedroom (and found it straight off, like a homing pigeon) while her class was looking at the mounds of potting soil in the leafless back garden. She entered the bed room quietly as though it was a place of worship, but then threw herself onto the bed with her arms outstretched as if it were her lover, lifted her hips and thrust them down into the sheets. The bed frame was wooden, nothing incriminating there. She breathed in the bed smell (laundry detergent, again nothing sordid) and browsed through the books on the small bedside table. *The Dialectic of Sex — the case for feminist revolution.*

The title was written in purple ink. She picked it up and smelled it, riffled through the pages, read the name at the front.

She wanted to drink the room through her skin, to bury its atmosphere deep inside the section of her brain called "heroine's bedroom and book list" so that she could think about it later while she played Patti Smith. She would never see any of this again. In the light of this, the room took on a nostalgic glow. Bonnie looked and looked. The walls were papered in tiny timid roses and a faint gold pinstripe; French windows led out onto a balcony. Some deeper, darker instinct made her wriggle snake-like to the edge of the bed and look under it. A large book with a pink cover lay half hidden by the fringe of the blanket. She reached under and pulled it out.

The Joy of Lesbian Sex, it was called. Her heart froze still and then knocked heavily at her ribs. She got up from the bed. She walked slowly downstairs. *Lesbian sex.* She stomped out into the garden and mingled with the others. A tree fern was about to be planted with great ceremony. *Lesbian sex, lesbian sex,* It was a litany that beat time with her heart. For a long time afterwards she associated the phrase with a tree fern sitting at the bottom of a soily hole.

"I was thinking of something a little less strong for the walls."

Bonnie felt Nora watch her closely for the rest of the evening. She got drunk and started speaking French. She sparkled in conversation and heard her voice lilting melodically. She laughed with a certain secret irony.

"My soul is stretched tightly across the skies," she said.

"Bonnie, don't talk shop," Sue Taylor said.

She spilt blackberry nip onto the seagrass matting in the spare room.

"Shit! I'm sorry."

But she wasn't, even though the stain was spreading in a large purple circle. Purple again.

Lesbian sex.

She snorted with a detective's triumph. Gasped for air.

"Bonnie," Sue Taylor hissed.

"It's OK. It'll come out," Nora took the glass out of her hand. "But I think you've had enough to drink."

"D'accord," she shrugged philosophically. "As-tu du cafe?"

At ten o'clock the English class left as it had arrived, in a large clump.

"It's been lovely. Thanks Nora." Jane spoke for all of them.

"That's fine. Study hard. Ring me if you have any problems."

They all walked in silence to the top of the street. Bonnie stopped, very suddenly. Nora's fingers had brushed hers as she reached to take her glass away. Sue Taylor turned and looked at her.

"You coming?"

"My mother's coming to pick me up," she said, slurring slightly. "From this very spot."

Sue looked closely at her. Her frilly shirt was accusing again, pointing tiny white ruffles at Bonnie. A tree next to them shivered with a small night breeze. It was straining to break through the pavement. Its large roots wanted to spread and spread.

"All right then. See you."

Bonnie sat down with a thump on the pavement. Her class disappeared from view. She regretted drinking so much. She regretted her boorish act. The rosewalled room and the large pink book had turned her from a stomping lumberjack into a seeker that had found the thing lost and then fumbled and dropped it. She was mourning something she'd never had.

At 10.30 she walked back to Nora's house and looked at the light in the lounge room. At 10.45 she knocked on the door. Endless minutes passed. Nora appeared. She held a dressing gown together with one hand.

"Hello, Bonnie."

Joy

"Hi! You know when you said ring me if you have any problems?"

She used the jollying tone of a salesman.

" ... yes. "

Bonnie couldn't see Nora's expression because the light was behind her. But her silhouette was relenting. It was being persuaded.

" ... well I forgot to get your number."

"I meant at school. Ring me at school."

"Can I use your toilet?"

Nora looked up and down the street and opened her door wider.

Lesbian sex.

"Come in."

Bonnie went to the bathroom and then the two of them sat in the lounge room in the hard wooden chairs and looked around the walls and bare floor. They were alone for the first time. Bonnie could smell soap very faintly. An oaty smell, not the traditional feminine roses or sweet frosty soap designed to disguise. Nora's hair was ringleted in wet curls around her neck. Her body had stood under a stream of water ten minutes ago, her breasts lathered and held and rinsed by the same hands that now sat demurely in Nora's lap. Maybe she was still wet beneath that dressing gown. Maybe steam was rising under there.

"Thanks for a lovely dinner tonight."

The six little words, small and inadequate ambassadors, bounced across the floorboards.

"What do you want, Bonnie?"

Such brusqueness could only mean that Nora knew. Bonnie got to her feet and walked across the floor that had recently been stripped of its carpet. She sat down next to her teacher, not to sell now but to convey. She felt like clearing her throat in anticipation. She watched herself with interest to see what her next move would be. She took Nora's hand. Ah!

Her hand is in my hand.

"I want to sleep with you."

Now her voice came out low and serious, because the sentence was mature and laden with huge capable words. It was a sentence loaded with history, laden with portent.

Nora looked down at Bonnie's hand and then picked it up and held it. And dropped it back in its owner's lap.

"You're drunk."

"I've been wanting to sleep with you for two years. This isn't something recent. This is long term."

Not that she knew what she was offering. The smell of oat soap was getting stronger as Nora grew heated and angry.

"You muck up in class all the time, you make stupid jokes. Is that how you try to impress me? Tonight you were an absolute idiot."

Bonnie made a note about tactics. Seduction required a certain grace.

"I was nervous. I wanted to impress you."

She wanted to say 'I'm the sort of person who doesn't do things. I am the sort of person who has things done to them. This is my first outing as a person. Notice it'.

"It didn't work. Sorry."

"Maybe you could reconsider," Bonnie suggested.

"I don't think so."

But to Bonnie, Nora sounded resigned, as if this were token resistance. Her hand had forgotten its job as guardian of the cordless gown. A portion of breast offered itself. Nora tried for the mundane.

"Do you have work lined up anywhere?"

"I'm starting work in a pet shop in January."

They both looked down at the floor. There was a silence while the word January floated around the room. Nora cleared her throat.

"I think you should go."

Bonnie looked down at her feet, put them together on the floor in order to propel herself to a standing position. She wondered why she felt no humiliation, and then she reasoned that she had fought the good fight. She had lost, that was all. She stood up and walked to the door. Nora opened it for her. A quaint politeness. They looked at each other as equals for the first time. There was the tinkling of the chime again. Bonnie cast around for something ironic to say. She opened her mouth just as Nora said:

"Look, I'm really attracted to you but it's just not possible."

"That's OK. I understand."

And then they kissed each other. A deep relaxed kiss now that both sides had conceded certain defeats. Every street sound was drowned out by the sound of the kiss and the sound of oxygen rushing through lips, cheeks. Bonnie's body was alert with adrenalin. She experienced the kiss from the other side of the room as if she were floating against the ceiling. She saw two women standing with their lips meeting, their jaws working. Arms were creeping round backs. One woman older, one younger. One leaning forward.

Nora pulled away suddenly.

"People can see in."

"I'd better come in then," said Bonnie the seducer.

They sank down onto the lounge and kissed again. Nora's breasts under the gown were soft and full. Nora broke away from the kiss suddenly.

"What am I doing? What the hell am I doing?"

And Bonnie comforted her. Kissed her neck, her throat, her hands. Moved her gently onto the wooden floor. Lay on her, pushed into her. Sat up to pull off her own shirt and lay back down. Felt breasts kiss against breasts for the first time. Nora nuzzled her lips against Bonnie's ear and said something that made her heart pound.

"Let's go upstairs."

The more steps she climbed, the more Bonnie's bravado wilted. She felt her desire seep away. Nora's back floated up and up and up the stairs in front of her. All right. That's enough, Bonnie thought. I just wanted to know if you liked me, that's all. Now that I know you do, I can go home.

She would have been happy to just sit next to Nora and thumb through books of poetry, swapping verse, analysing mildly. But it was too late. The audience of timid roses trembled on their paper stems. *The Joy of Lesbian Sex* flared in a puddle of pink on the floor next to Nora's dressing gown. Nora, naked and shivering, pulled off Bonnie's jeans with difficulty.

"What are these made of? Old army tents?"

They sank into each other slowly as though they were drowning in a warm current that prevented sudden movement.

All this foreign skin.

"Relax," Nora murmured. "You're really tense."

She reached down and rubbed a palm over Bonnie's nipples.

"Mm."

9

Her hand slid down further. Bonnie kissed Nora and felt the ache in her groin start up again. But she knew she would not come. She was surprised how easy it was to make someone else gasp and thrust with pleasure while her own body and mind lay unmoved.

Cells in her body asked, hey, who is this next to us? They shrank from contact. They had lived too long on their own to split and form new lives. But her newly appointed diplomat hands went on to boldly explore foreign parts and move like experts until Nora lay calm and breathing like a coiled spring that's finally been unwound and unwound. The air in the room hung suspended.

Was that it? Bonnie wanted to ask.

Nora looked at her sheepishly.

"I wasn't much use to you, was I?"

Bonnie mumbled into the sheet. "First time, that's all."

Nora rolled Bonnie towards her. Their breasts tipped and nudged like old friends.

"Next time will be better."

Bonnie nodded, believing. She looked down at the union that was suggested by their joined bodies. She looked at the nipples of her former teacher. Roan colt. They lay next to each other, as coy as two debutantes.

"Do you know anything about me? Did you know I was a lesbian?"

Bonnie frowned with the lack of an answer. If she had known anything about Nora the obsession would not have been as exciting. She couldn't say that. Nor could she say that Miss Driver was the sixth teacher that Bonnie had fallen in love with. And in her fantasies, Nora was all over her, so of course she was a lesbian.

Nora didn't wait for an answer. She started telling a story in a bright story-telling voice.

"I remember the first time I ever kissed a woman. I was saying good night to my best friend on the front verandah. We'd gone to school together years before and we kept in touch. She and her husband had come over for dinner."

"Did you live here then?"

Bonnie needed a setting.

"No. Anyway, he said goodbye to me and went and waited next to the car. He was opening the doors. I gave her a peck on the cheek and then our mouths met —"

"Met?"

"Well, by accident, sort of, and I kissed her properly."

"What did she do?"

"She kissed me back."

'What did the husband do?"

Bonnie was dragging her fingers down Nora's back.

"He didn't know. He was sitting in the driver's seat by then. He had the radio on."

"What song was on?"

Nora thought for a minute.

"Roy Orbison. 'Pretty Woman'."

"Didn't he —"

"There was no verandah light."

"Ah. And then what?"

" She put her arms around me and we kept kissing. I was incredibly excited."

Painful detail. Hurry it along. "And then?"

"After a while she pulled away from me and walked down the steps. She turned and waved from the road."

Bonnie watched her teacher lift her arm from the bed and mime a wave.

"Did she say anything?"

"She said 'Don't forget you've still got my casserole dish!'"

"How stupid!"

"She just meant: 'That kiss didn't mean anything but I still want to be friends with you.'"

"That's awful."

"No it wasn't. Don't forget I had a boyfriend at the time. I didn't think about it again until days later and then I couldn't stop thinking about it. So I took over her casserole dish."

"Did anything happen?"

"Did we have sex? No. I asked her and she turned me down. Turned me out, I should say. Right out of her house."

Bonnie chewed at the top sheet, struggling between jealousy and sympathy.

"You poor thing." But it sounded flat.

"Just remember never to get involved with married women. You know what she did? She wrote to me and said 'Nora, I think marriage is your best option'."

"How old were you?"

"Twenty two. It was five years ago."

Five years? Was that all? Bonnie knew when she had first known. In primary school she used to draw pictures of naked women whose breasts stood out large and firm. She remembered one vision that she couldn't get right on paper, even though she worked at it for ages with a fetishist's eye for perfection and detail. She wanted to draw two women kissing but her efforts made them look like sexless Siamese twins joined at the lips. How did you draw passion? She knew only how to stomp it out on the floor of her room.

The pictures were quickly sketched in pencil and then rubbed out, or hidden. Mostly hidden. She hated to throw them out because they represented too much. Drawing hands had been the hardest thing. She remembered fantasies of cuddling women that turned sexual, kissing that somehow involved the whole body in delicious frisson.

When she rode home from school on the bus she looked at the breasts of women sitting opposite. Of course it was best when she sat staring abstractly at nothing except the innocent breathing chests of women standing in front of her. The rise and fall, the wave beneath the cloth that jigged backwards and forwards. She may have been contemplating homework with a glazed frown. On the beach she became an expert in the casual glance while talking to her friends.

Nora fell asleep quickly but Bonnie lay awake in the dark, aroused and sleepless. She had taken some huge step in the last hour. She knew that she would wake up a different person, as though sleep was the time when voices broke, wrinkles were added to the face and new identities slipped over the body and soul like a second skin.

*

Bonnie moved in and helped Nora renovate the house. She felt as though she had won a fantastic prize. A prize too fragile to hold up to the light and too precious to throw away. Bonnie waited for the moment when it would all come clear and she would know how to proceed in conversations with Nora. To ward off timidity they painted the lounge room walls and dug in a fish pond next to the tree fern. They covered bare boards. Bonnie brought fat orange goldfish home from the pet shop. They went to nurseries and to the Botanic Gardens and Nora made her repeat the names of plants while their bodies steamed together in the light of various glasshouses.

"Polypodium, lycopodium, adiantum."

She nibbled Nora's ear. The house became a jungle of plants, the names of which Bonnie could recite to Nora's friends.

They went to her mother's for Sunday dinners of red cabbage and sausage. The first time she introduced them to each other, Bonnie's stomach cramped with anxiety.

"Nora this is my mother Clara. Mum, this is Nora."

But they said hello and her mother made them coffee. They drank it and went home. She felt relieved but what had she expected to happen? She was scared Nora would disappear in a puff of smoke. The house was so full of the fantasy Nora that maybe the real Nora would be wispy and insubstantial. But she sat easily at the table. The straight line that was Bonnie sitting at one end and Clara at the other became an equal-sided triangle with no fuss at all.

Sunday nights became a cosy tradition for the three of them; there was a celebratory tang in the air, as though something great and worthwhile had been accomplished.

Her mother rang them to remind them of dinner, sat them down to it as soon as they arrived and put parcels of food in their car when they left. Nora would shake her head while she drove: "I'm just amazed at the way your mother accepts us. My mother won't even talk about it. And all that food!"

At night they lay like innocents in bed. They went to movies together to stave off the silences. Then one Monday Nora came home and her face was pale. She was stiff with shock.

"What's up? What's wrong?"

Nora sank onto the lounge and squeezed her hands together.

"A Fourth form girl came up to me after class and said 'I saw you on Sunday, Miss. You were in George Street, holding hands with someone'." She smeared a hand over her face. "The way she said it. Someone."

"Would I know her?"

Nora didn't hear.

"We're going to have to stop."

"Stop what?"

"Everything. We're going to have to be careful."

It was as though someone had thrown a dun-coloured blanket over their lives. Nora grew more anxious while Bonnie grumbled more and more. They went out less and less.

"Who's that?" Nora would ask suddenly as they were driving along. "Put your head down, quick!"

Bonnie ducked down, her head almost in Nora's lap.

"You know this would look pretty bad. If someone happened to look in the window. In fact it would look ten times worse than us just driving along together. People do ride in cars together. It doesn't mean they're having sex."

But Nora had stopped listening as well as breathing.

"This is the last time I'm doing this," Bonnie swore to herself.

Nora drove on, her mouth thin as string.

"You can get up now."

"Who was it anyway?"

"It was Andrew Bain."

"Who the hell is Andrew Bain?"

"The new science teacher."

"Jesus, Nora, he doesn't even know me!"

"Doesn't matter. You look like a high school student."

Their lives hung suspended.

It changed everything except their sex life, which never improved anyway.

The Joy of Lesbian Sex disappeared after their first night together and Bonnie didn't mention it for fear that Nora would be hurt. And because she was shy. They were bound by cords of shyness. She and Nora were attempting to speak the same language but the dictionaries they used were different. The two goldfish that wriggled fatly in eternal circles around the mud-brown pond reminded Bonnie of her and Nora. She sat next to the water and watched them for hours, looking for clues.

"Nora," she told them one day "I think we should break up."

*

Nora and Bonnie kept their Sunday night routine at Clara's place but Nora now drove Bonnie to her bedsit in Darlinghurst and give her a chaste kiss goodnight. Without the pressure of a relationship they found themselves chatting to each other easily. Clara knew they had broken up but for some reason wanted to pretend they hadn't.

"She's the reverse of most mothers. She wants a dyke for a daughter. She's scared I'll sleep with some man and fall pregnant."

Nora almost immediately started seeing Melanie. Bonnie approved of Melanie. She was a potter with a weakness for funk with bass lines that popped right off the record. She had loudspeakers out on her lawn and she didn't care that neighbours hung their heads over the fence and asked her to turn it down.

"Who the hell's this?" Bonnie asked one day.

"Stanley Clarke. Greatest living bass guitarist. Do you like it?"

"Yep."

It was the best stuff she'd heard since Patti Smith. She didn't know why Melanie would work in stodgy sticky clay when she knew about this sort of music. Her whole appearance was at right angles to her personality.

Melanie had a studio in her garden. Pieces of reddish clay littered the lawn around an old stone birdbath. When Bonnie first saw the garden she offered to remove the clay for her.

"I'll get my mate Belle's ute. Wouldn't take long."

Melanie smiled.

"I like them there, actually."

"It's art work, you dodo," Nora said.

Bonnie peered closely at one of the bits of clay and saw that it was a tiny mushroom.

"Oh yeah."

"That's the vegetable section," Melanie said. "Over here are my tropical fruits." Further back against the fence was a cluster of miniature pineapples, melons and mangoes.

"Oh yeah," said Bonnie and dug up a horseshoe of earth with the heel of her boot. Visual art made her tongue-tied.

Melanie was serious but chatty. She wanted people to know what she thought and wanted to know what they thought back. She and Nora bickered constantly. They finished each other's sentences, read each other's minds and drove each mad. Nora complained that Melanie was obsessed with her potting which meant that Melanie didn't pay her enough attention. Nora started going to clowning workshops. Bonnie dropped around one day and found Melanie sitting at the potting wheel, her hands cupped around spinning wet clay.

"Where's Nor?"

"She's getting in touch with her inner clown," Melanie shouted above the sound of the wheel. She didn't crack a smile or raise an eyebrow, which showed great loyalty Bonnie thought. She sat down and watched Melanie's fingers carve long elegant lines into the wet clay. Melanie had run out of things to say and Bonnie was about to get up and awkwardly leave when Nora appeared.

"Found your clown yet?" Bonnie asked.

Nora dropped into a cane chair and looked at her. The sunlight showed up the fine lines around her mouth and eyes.

"When you're my age, you'll understand what this is all about."

Nora kept going to clown school. After ten months she could juggle, do somersaults and stand on her head in the middle of the room for long periods. She found her inner clown. She was called Jessie.

"Where did you find her?" Bonnie asked. "Grace Brothers?"

"Your laughter does nothing but spur me on," Nora said.

Now she was looking younger. She resigned from teaching. She sold her house with the tree fern and pond and moved in with Melanie. She grew her hair out into a comfortable mane around her shoulders. She stopped wearing the leather jacket that Bonnie loved. All her new clothes were bright and bouncy. Kiddies clothes. She slept her mornings away and clowned in the afternoon.

Bonnie watched this change with sorrow. This was the woman who she could have gone out with two years ago. They could have walked down the street as bold as brass, Nora in her bright reds and greens and yellows, Bonnie in more sober black and white. One day Nora turned up on Bonnie's door step.

"Melanie and I had a fight. She told me she was missing her space."

For an instant Bonnie thought she meant outer space and she saw Melanie floating around the galaxy with her pots, Nora clutching an ankle. Nora walked into the kitchen and filled the kettle.

"What happened?"

"She shouted out 'You're upsetting my pots'. Not 'You're upsetting me!' but 'you're upsetting my pots!' Don't you think that's weird? God this kitchen's tiny. You couldn't swing a bachelor in it."

"You got violent?" Bonnie was shocked.

Nora looked sheepish.

"I thought I was over my Saturn return."

"Don't bring astrology into this. You're just a moody old bag."

"Have I always been?"

Nora was in one of her pathetic moods.

"Look at my foot! I think it's broken."

She wriggled it out of its sandal and flopped it into Bonnie's lap.

"What am I? Your doctor?"

"Oh Bon, I forgot. I nicked this for you."

She pulled an object from her rucksack and plumped it into Bonnie's hand like prize booty. It was a tiny clay pineapple.

"I knew you liked these."

Bonnie looked at her. Nora had a lopsided smile.

"I never did apologise for our rotten sex life," she said.

Bonnie stroked the baby spikes and rubbed the rough clay that looked deceptively smooth.

Sweet but inedible.

2

Bonnie didn't sleep with anyone. She returned to loving women from a distance, addicted to the unprovable theory of unrequited love. University provided a bumper crop of strong silent types. She'd moved into a ground floor bedsit in Darlinghurst and worshipped them silently. She studied, learned how to interpret texts, learned how to smoke dope, buy it and roll it, how to talk about theories and how to pretend she knew more than she did. She wore overalls dyed purple and made money cleaning offices three nights a week.

Living alone was interesting. But she was easily distracted. She would walk into the bathroom to clean her teeth and remember a word she wanted to look up. She walked out of the bathroom and over to the book shelf. Once there she would see a book she hadn't read for a while, pick it up, leaf through it. Start to read. Then she felt the scum on her enamel. She needed to clean her teeth. Back to the bathroom which looked familiar. Recent. And then she remembered the sequence of events. It was frightening how easy it was to wander.

Her desk and bed shook when trucks roared down Crown Street. At night she heard the sad tap tap of a toothbrush being hit against a sink in the flat above her. The water pipes in the walls became slow shuddering beats in her head. While she prepared essays her tongue and teeth clicked them out and ground them into exotic cross rhythms. Again she sat up on her bed and her right foot started.

At the end of her final year she took up drumming.

Well finally! something in her said.

"Why drums?" people asked her.

She tried to justify it, although a finer instinct said no don't justify, as long as you know why. You don't have to justify your pleasures to people. Even to people who were genuinely curious she couldn't explain. Drumming was simple and intricate, and some sort of power. It pulsed in her. It drove her. It made life easy. It fell into place in her life. It was the only thing that appealed. She was twenty two.

She took lessons from a jazz drummer who didn't need to ask her why she was interested. His name was Charlie.

"I don't want you to even look at a real drum kit for two months," Charlie said sternly.

His other pupils were young boys full of zeal who would rush out, she imagined, and buy drums straight off. Charlie played in a quartet at the Hilton and wore an aftershave that smelled of insecticide. He made lessons with him sound like a plan of battle. She liked that.

"You'll learn how to hold your sticks first. They have to become an extension of your arms. Use your fingers as support for the rebound. See? Like this."

He dropped the tip of the drumstick onto the rubber. It bounced back, and back again, and back again, without any movement from his arm. His fingers cradled the butt end of the wood.

"It's in the wrist. And the fingers."

She gawked.

"And now a roll."

The sticks became blurs of wood and air. It seemed effortless. The sound of wood against rubber was a purr.

Her blood raced as she walked into the city. She had been given the key to a secret society. Music shops were a different prospect. Musicians were her brothers and sisters now. She listened to the songs blaring from shops and cars and stored rhythms in her head. Drumming was a miracle and she would learn its secrets. Her life had found a road.

After four months she bought a drum kit from a woman whose boyfriend had gone to England. They stood and looked at the heap of drums on the floor.

"I don't know what it's worth. You can have the whole lot for 200 bucks." The woman looked at Bonnie's overalls. "I'll chuck in a pair of jeans as well if you want."

She politely refused the jeans and drove her treasure home in Clara's car. She spread the pieces out over the floor. Like an encyclopaedia learner, she knew the names of all the parts before she ever saw them — bass drum, foot pedal, snare drum, one hanging tom, a floor tom, two cymbals, hi hat.

She pulled the actual drums apart, removed the steel rims from the dark red shells with a drum key, lifted off their skins gently. She oiled everything that was metal, wiped down everything that was plastic and polished everything wooden. She reassembled it all and took photos from different angles. She put the circle of black rubber on the snare drum.

"And now a roll," she said and tried one. She put her right foot gingerly on the bass drum pedal and played a four four beat. She stopped. A spring on the bass drum pedal was squeaking. She got down on her hands and knees and oiled it. She tried it with her hand. Boomp! Boomp. Better.

She played her rudiments with the bass drum banging along. She practised for three hours. Neighbours thumped on the wall.

"Let's get your whole body working," Charlie said at the beginning of the next lesson. "You have a full kit, so let's see how you use it."

He cleared his throat.

"OK. In drumming music the stave is used as a ladder for the different parts of the kit. The bass drum sits on one line, this one here." He tapped the page. "The snare drum sits on another line, here. Ride cymbal and crash cymbal here on the top. To play any sort of rhythm from a chart, you have to follow all the lines and know what's going on with every part of the kit. Accents are marked and rests are marked just like in ordinary charts. You have to learn how to read the way ahead as well."

In the little back room, separated from other students by plywood walls, Bonnie learned to play the ride cymbal on automatic pilot. Her right arm ached but the cymbal pattern didn't falter. Her right foot pushed out the one and three on the bass drum pedal. Her entire body was stretched, as though she were a rock climber halfway up a cliff. Arms and legs clung perilously to crevices and pockets in the rock. To let go now would be to fall to the silence waiting below. Her deltoids ached, her calf muscle ached but her skeleton commanded a continuum. She was playing a rock beat. She was the rock beat. Sweat rolled down her face. She didn't breathe. Don't stop, her body commanded. Her shoulders rose with the strain. They started to hurt.

"No! Shoulders down!" cried her teacher. She relaxed them without faltering for a second. The last bar on the page was approaching. She played it. She stopped.

"Good," he said. "Take a break before you explode."

She let out the breath she'd been holding in a long loud rush.

"The other important thing is to relax while you concentrate. You have to physically relax. That's the important part of playing."

Bonnie bought books. She ground out rhythms with her teeth between clenched jaws, quietly. She learnt how to play rudiments – hand to hand rolls, two stroke rolls. Flams that spread the beat and made it fat. Paradiddles. It was all so simple. You practised and you improved. Each exercise was poetry in its form and economy.

Left right left left. Right left right right.

She practised for hours on a small rubber pad. She drummed on the table while she ate.

"Is this going to be a career?" Clara asked one day. She was on her way to lunch at a friend's place in Paddington, someone Bonnie hadn't met. Bonnie divided her mother's friends into categories of before Dad left and after Dad left. The after Dads always had male acquaintances for her mother to meet.

"Or is it just one of your fantasies?"

Her mother had a clearer idea of her fantasies than she would have liked.

"I don't know."

Outside was the gentler hum of Sunday traffic.

"Do you love playing this thing?"

"Yes."

Clara leaned back then.

"Well, that's something."

Her mother loved stories of talented people who triumphed against disastrous odds. Bonnie remembered her stories of the world's creators, mad but visioned. Poor but famous. Male but not female. Her mother stroked a cymbal.

"These are beautiful. Are they brass?"

Bonnie nodded. She had spent precious money on cymbal cleaner and polished them till they glowed. Their quality reassured her mother.

"Maybe you'll be a classical player one day. Maybe you'll play the timpani. Remember your father and I used to take you to see the Sydney Symphony at the Town Hall? You were about eight."

Bonnie remembered resting her chin on the warm dark wood and hoping the huge organ wasn't going to play. Its pipes loomed above everything and its noise would be the blast from an ocean liner – terrifying, enormous. The orchestra tuned fussily. Everyone was in black and white. The conductor came out in his much crisper black and white. He bowed. After a delicious agony-filled silence the music started to come out from everywhere.

One man stood in front of a drum – a snare drum she now knew – and played a little rumpety tump every now and then. He held his drumsticks as though they were soup spoons. The other instruments waited for him in silence and then played the tune again as if to remind him.

She remembered that now. He had looked so happy. The innocence of the little repeating rhythm and the way the music rose and fell, loud then soft then loud, pierced her heart and she'd hidden tears way down in the back of her nose and throat. She wanted to keep it to herself and not have to explain. She froze in her seat and looked down at her hands twined in her lap, feeling the world until it hurt.

*

Belle sat on the bed constructing a cigarette.

"I do not roll joints. I do not roll cigarettes," she often said "I *build* them. See this." She held out a joint like a trumpet.

Belle made smoking an occasion. She made everything an occasion. Going for a quick drink was an occasion for Belle. Going to class every day was an occasion. Even as a student she had worn beautiful shirts and expensive trousers, as though she were preparing for the day when fame would suddenly pounce and her worth would be recognised in the public arena. She looked like a modern day Radclyffe Hall, all blazers and silk shirts. She was Bonnie's first real lesbian friend.

She liked to work with people and she liked to be watched. As she watched Bonnie, now she frowned.

"When are you going to go out in the real world and make some money from this drumming business?"

Belle associated a creative skill with income. She had majored in film theory. She was the best film maker at university by third year and now she was working her way up. Belle knew exactly what she wanted. Her sense of purpose rang clear and loud. She would be a director. She was determined.

Bonnie also felt determined but she had bad days. Days when she saw herself in ten years time still borrowing cars. Driving to RSL clubs. She imagined setting up the drum kit, slowed by arthritis. There would be a crowd requesting, 'Golden Wedding'. Bonnie would sit at the back of the stage, her right foot pumping away, her right hand swatting the rhythm on the ride cymbal as couples shuffled in an eternal circle.

But today was not a bad day.

"It's not a business, it's an art. I'll play in public when I can play properly."

Belle lay back and kissed smoke at the ceiling. It floated up in elegant rings. Bonnie played a sequence of paradiddles on her rubber pad. Right right left right. Left left right left. She increased speed until the sticks were a blur chasing away the small flat and the Golden Wedding. The roll faltered. Then back to slow. Her right foot beat in four.

"Are you seeing anyone at the moment?" Belle asked.

"I haven't got time."

"I know someone who likes you."

Her trousered left leg swung back and forth.

Right right left right.

"I'm married to my music."

Left left right left.

"When was the last time you had sex?"

"Hey?"

"Sex. Are you familiar with it? Drumming's fine but you're not a bloody nun. Sex is something that shouldn't be sublimated. Especially for women like us."

"Us? You mean lesbians?"

"Of course. We need to propagate our identity. Didn't you learn this stuff at uni? Do you want some of this before it goes out?"

It was an ember between her fingers.

"I must have missed Lesbian One. I was studying literary theory instead."

Bonnie spoke flatly to her little rubber pad. She realised that she had chosen music over sex somehow. When had that happened?

"Don't you think that sex would be beneficial to your music?"

People said music when they meant rhythm. Or was it music? Bonnie wasn't sure. Being not sure was a familiar feeling.

"Why? Beethoven didn't have sex for years."

"Why? Because he was deaf?"

"Maybe. Anyway, Virginia Woolf didn't have sex."

"That's crap." Belle stood up and ground out the stub of joint. "I'm going to find someone for you."

Belle was like her mother, wanting her to join some world of her own making. She walked to the door and picked up her car keys.

Bonnie held out her hands, palms up.

"Hey Belle! Look at my blisters."

As if hours of lonely practice were proof of something. She looked at her practice pad. There were two white ovals where her sticks had bounced up and down, again and again.

*

Bonnie got a phone call from someone called Simon. He was a director. He'd heard she was a drummer. Could she perhaps play in Wastelandish Theatre's next production? She knew the Wastelandish Theatre. It was out in the industrial heart of the city. Its plays were ideologically sound; powerful, dramatic missiles of moral instruction. Its musicals were spiced with jolly chorus lines and determined Australian accents. Filled with messages.

This play was called *Naked City*. Purely amateur of course, but then she played drums because she loved it, right? Three weeks rehearsal and then performances every Friday, Saturday and Sunday for a six week season. Unpaid glory but glory. What did she say to that? She said, "You haven't even heard me play."

Suspicious that someone wanted her.

But she was also dancing with delight. The world had beckoned her to join it. She shifted from one foot to the other, impatient to get off the phone and reflect upon this new development. Outside her window the sky was blossoming with interesting late afternoon light.

"Come in for the next rehearsal on Sunday and we'll run through a couple of scenes."

"My reading's lousy."

"It's atmospheric drumming we want. You'll be improvising. There're no charts. Please say yes!"

"How did you get my name?"

"I know your friend Belle."

Everyone knew Belle.

"OK, I'll do it."

She hung up.

On Sunday Bonnie loaded her drums into Clara's car.

"We're going out to play, kids."

She drove to the Wastelandish while her bass drum rolled back and forward across the back seat. The Wastelandish squatted on the kerb of the main highway. From the street it seemed identical to the sober little brick-red post office next door. On the other side was a petrol station which Bonnie never saw open the whole time she was there.

She banged on the double doors. There was the ominous noise of bolts being drawn and then a man came out and blinked against the sunlight. Behind him it was pitch black. He finally seemed to see her.

"You the drummer?"

She nodded. He stared at her for longer than was necessary, and just when she thought he was about to say 'don't I know you from somewhere?' he scooped her drums up like boxes of candy and carried them inside. Muscles stood out on his neck. Bonnie picked up the cymbals and followed him.

"I'm Bonnie," she said to his back.

"Forwards," he said.

How rude, Bonnie thought.

He climbed a flight of stairs past the empty box office and then stopped suddenly.

"Muso's here," he called into the dark. A light came on above their heads. Bonnie saw that she stood at the top of an empty auditorium.

Not quite empty. A group of naked men sat in a circle at the front of the stage. A voice floated up.

"Bonnie?"

She couldn't see.

"Come down here. This is the drummer everyone."

The naked men watched her make a slow, stumbling descent to the foot of the stage. The rude man in the jeans dumped her cases on a small riser at the left of the stage. A shadow sitting in the third row grabbed her arm, patted a seat with the other hand and sat her gently in it. She saw a thatch of blond hair so white it glowed in the dark.

"Come sit here. Just till we finish this scene. I'm Simon." He pumped her hand and dropped it. He turned back to the stage. "From your line Billy!"

The overhead light went out.

One of the men stood slowly and faced the auditorium. Bonnie thought that it had been a long time since she had seen a penis. And never in the sort blue light that was illuminating this one from all directions. She tried not to stare, even though the darkness hid her curiosity.

"I reckon we stay and FIGHT," the man said. He curled his hand into a fist and raised it in the air. "If we run, we'll LOSE our source of FOOD."

"That's true," one of the sitting men said. He looked pale.

"Louder, James."

"THAT'S TRUE," the pale man said and coughed. He curled his hand protectively around his crotch.

"Sorry," he said "can I talk it through just for now?"

"Fishermen's Friends, James. Live on them. You've got Scene Two to do yet. Carry on."

"That's true. Our only water supply is right here." He leaned down and tapped something invisible on the floorboards.

"Forwards, give us a bucket of water or something!"

"Is that his name?" Bonnie asked, comprehension dawning.

"Economy of speech as well as movement. Never says more than four words at a time."

"Oh I see! Four Words!"

He looked down at her with a bucket in his hand.

"What?"

"Carry on," Simon said.

She watched the scene with bewilderment. They were planning some sort of raid on something. Why were the men naked? Simon's voice came out of the dark again.

"I suppose you're wondering why they're naked."

"Yes."

"It's symbolic, not to be taken literally. They've been stripped of all they have. They're at their most primitive state. In this play man has hit rock bottom! You better set your drum kit up."

She tiptoed around onto the stage and positioned her drums on the riser. She hauled out a stool from the dressing room. Above the kit a red light slowly flashed on and off. The men had finished their scene now, and wandered around, chatting and drinking coffee. Dicks everywhere, thought Bonnie. But not to be taken literally. One or two of the older men put underpants on. There was a certain irony here that she would have enjoyed more if she wasn't sick with nerves. The stage set looked like a ruined city. Dick Land.

Simon stood up from his seat and clapped his hands together.

"Scene Two, everyone!"

This time only one man walked on to the stage.

"Now, Bonnie. This scene is extremely angry. James is not only mourning the death of his wife, he is swearing to revenge her killing. He is promising bloodshed. The mood is angry! Do you understand?"

She nodded. Yes, of course she understood anger.

"So, the drums must be angry. But!" Simon held up a forefinger. "There is an underlying sadness, as well. A poignancy behind the bravado. Do you think you can provide a feel for that?"

He was smiling at her, willing her response. The man's a wanker, she thought.

"I'll try."

He clapped his hands.

"OK!"

James stood alone on stage under a blue light. A white body length piece of sacking was on the floor next to him. Bonnie sat behind the drum kit, her palms sweating. She could see only the back of James' head. She felt a strange bond with him, as though an elastic band of terror held them suspended together. Simon and the cast were sprawled across various seats looking interested. Even if she determined not to look at them, Simon's platinum hair shone like a beacon. She was so nervous her sticks shook. Why? Because she was not a real drummer, that's why. What if her drums didn't make any noise? She would faint. She was a fraud. What if her arms wouldn't move? She would —

A soft red light came up as though to soothe her.

"Action!"

Her arms moved of their own accord and rolled a low rumble on the floor tom. It became American Indian in feel, an accented four four beat that was slow and threatening. James started to circle the stage. He looked at her, his face a mask of shock. She almost stopped but realised he was looking through her at something else. He stopped his pacing and threw his head back.

"Auugh!"

Bonnie dropped it down a bit.

"Look at her!"

He pointed to the floor. "Look at her lying there. Why don't I just plunge a knife into my own sorry flesh and end it now?"

"Why should I live? She is dead! My life is dead!"

Small pieces of red came flying out of his mouth.

Swelling cymbal.

"We have held back. We have not killed, we have not sought revenge." His face grew hard and angry. "But I swear!"

Back to floor tom. Low roll. Sustained. She was on the cliff face again, clinging to whatever her fingers and toes could find. Don't look down.

"I will see them die for what they have done. I will see their water poisoned and their limbs hacked!"

Don't stop. Another shower of red spittle.

What was wrong with him?

25

"Ah, the thought is so sweet! Yes ... " He closed his eyes to savour the sweetness and started to pace again.

"Death to the killers of women!"

They were in a rhythm now, her and James. The drums underlined. Dramatised. Her footing was surer. She would not fall. Her hands on the toms gave his words thundering acclaim. A resounding roll around the kit.

"And black!" shouted Simon.

There was total darkness. Bonnie's last beat echoed through the hall, then there was silence. She sat, breathing fast.

James stood clutching his throat.

"Are you all right?" she whispered.

"Sore throat." he croaked.

"Were you spitting blood just then?"

He shook his head.

"Throat lozenges."

The lights came up. Simon and the cast had got to their feet and were clapping. James reached over and gripped her hand for a second.

"Well done," he whispered.

Simon leapt onto the stage.

"Absolutely fantastic! James, do the drums lift the scene or what?"

James nodded.

"I think he's sick," Bonnie said.

"Are you sick?"

James nodded again.

"All right. Sit down. We'll do Billy's bit. Bonnie, Scene Five has more drumming. James can fill you in on it. Billy!"

More handclapping. A young muscular man walked onto stage centre. He looked sullen, but in the manner of handsome boys, it may have been the awkwardness of physical beauty not yet grown into. Someone wolf-whistled quietly. Someone else gave a sighing sort of moan and there was a low snigger of laughter from the cast. Billy ignored them. He stood and owned the stage, his chin lifted.

Bonnie and James sat together in the stalls.

"It was fantastic you know? I didn't know what the hell I was going to play. It just happened. Fantastic. Off the top of my head."

James smiled at her. She was raving, she realised, but she didn't want to break their connection. She needed to talk. She could think of changes already to improve the dynamics.

"So! What's Scene Five about?"

James looked surprised.

"You don't doe?" he whispered. She could hear his lungs rattling.

"No. Tell me."

"Dove seed." he wheezed and coughed.

"What's dove seed?"

He shook his head and pointed at Billy and then at his own chest.

"Love scene."

"Oh."

James blew his nose loudly.

"My favourite scene. Actually, Simon should base the whole play around him and call it Billy's Buns. The boy is a *god.*" He stopped for a second, held up an apologetic hand and sneezed dramatically. "They're what'll carry it through. Ad your superb drumming, of course."

He thrust a cellophane bag at her. "Lozenge?"

Later that night Belle rang her.

"How was it?"

"Like first day at primary school."

But glorious.

3

On the night that Belle threw a party, there was the merest hint of winter in the air. It was the middle of April, when days were still brilliant blue but the nights were crisp. The changes in climate did not disturb the grit that settled daily on Bonnie's shelves and window ledges, nor did she notice it particularly. The only dirt she disturbed was the dust she tapped her fingers on absent-mindedly.

Belle came over in the afternoon and peered through the window. Bonnie sat at the drum kit eating a cheese sandwich.

"You're not wearing those bloody overalls tonight, Bonnie."

"You're not choosing my clothes for me!"

"If you wear those I'm disowning you."

"Then I'm not going."

But she crammed the bread in her mouth and opened the front door. Belle walked to the wardrobe, searched through Bonnie's clothes and threw a pair of black jeans on the bed.

"Try these on when you've unpursed your lips."

"They're too hot. And too tight."

Working in the theatre had given Bonnie a certain feistiness.

"So? They're hot and tight. It's only for a couple of hours."

Belle unclipped Bonnie's overall buckles and pushed her back on the bed.

"Did you ever want to sleep with me, Belle?"

"It's crossed my mind."

"Why didn't you say anything?"

"Because I know you. You would have run a mile. You're all theory, no practice. Apart from your drumming."

Bonnie took off her T shirt and picked up the black jeans. Belle fixed her gaze carefully at the window as if her next question was directed at something on the footpath outside.

"Anyway, would you have said yes?"

Bonnie looked at herself in the mirror and raised her eyebrows. She sucked in her stomach.

"Hey, these jeans don't look half bad!"

"Don't overwhelm me with passion. Let's go."

*

"The woman who likes you is here tonight but I'm not telling you who it is."

"What's the point in that?"

"Feel the situation, Bon. Feel it here." Belle tapped her stomach.

"Stop directing me."

"You'll know her when you see her."

Bonnie sat in the hall way and took out her packet of Drum. Pretended not to look around while she licked papers together. It was the crucial moment when the paper ends had to curve towards each other, touch and then overlap.

"Bonnie?"

Her tobacco fell out as she looked up. It was Serena holding two cans of beer. *Was it Serena?*

"You're in some play aren't you? How's it going?"

"It's great. I sit under a red light and play anything I like. I reflect the emotions on stage. Six blokes and me. I love it."

"Oh ..."

"No, I'm serious ... it's fantastic!"

She took a beer from Serena and swigged.

"I was taking that to someone."

"Oops." She shook the beer can. "Some left. D'you want it back?"

"God you're uncouth! Finish it, I'll get another one."

So Bonnie sat on the floor and smoked and finished the beer. And when people tripped on her feet they apologised, which was conversation of a sort. She imagined Nora and Melanie wandering around the party.

'Eugh! Too much smoke' they'd say as the party screamed on around them. Bonnie finished her beer and looked around Belle's lounge room. God. Film people everywhere. Terrifying. They wore the clothes of the materially impoverished but the creatively enriched. Earrings curved and glittered. Black denim was ripped, T shirts were hand painted with stark designs and slogans. Only one woman wore a dress. There were mohawks which looked primly coiffed next to the raggedy lesbian ducks ass.

Bonnie looked at the woman in the dress. Other people were looking at her too, she noticed. But they were sneaking looks as if they weren't supposed to. The woman was talking to a man in a white shirt and black vest but her body stood in a stiff posture that said to the room 'I know you are watching me'. Her hair was nothing spectacular: short, brown, wavy but not especially so. It was an afterthought frame for the startling, beautiful face. She did nothing dramatic with her body but she radiated something.

Bonnie watched her head tilt one way and then another. Her eyebrows registered surprise, then amusement and her floral dress swirled in small movements. She was a professional listener at a dull party. She started to

29

shift from one foot to the other. She nodded to the man more times than she answered him.

The woman looked around the room as though she were seeking someone out. She kept pushing her hair back from her forehead. The gesture was very small and sad. She glanced at Bonnie. Their eyes locked for a second. Then the woman's gaze travelled on. Bonnie felt her body glow with the unmistakable heat of interest. She looked inside her empty beer can. Right into the hole, as if she could see something interesting.

"Something down there?"

Belle was at her elbow.

"Belle, do you know that woman over there?"

Belle followed Bonnie's eyes and snorted with amusement.

"Bon! Everyone knows her."

"Why?"

"She's famous! You must know her."

Bonnie saw a face in her mind and the name of a film swam its way to the surface. Her heart sank. A famous woman whose identity was artificial, not natural.

An actress.

"She played the widow in *Crossing the Heart?*"

She and Nora had seen it during the first glow of romance.

"Yep."

"She's beautiful."

Belle put a hand on Bonnie's shoulder.

"Everyone falls in love with her because she has that sad look. People love it."

They stood and watched her.

"See the way her hand curves down and around like that, sort of hanging from her wrist? Only a straight woman would do that. The whole posture. It screams heterosexual. She has the look of straight women who are protected."

"Her hair's quite short."

"That doesn't mean anything any more."

"So you've worked with her?"

"Yep. I'll introduce you to her." Belle started to pull Bonnie along.

"No, I don't think so."

"Belle!"

The woman walked towards them. People still watched her out of the corners of their eyes. Was she ever not watched? She stood in front of them. Bonnie ground her teeth nervously but then stopped. It made the muscles in her jaw move around, and it looked like she had a nervous tic or a mouth full of toffee.

"Bonnie, this is Angela Corbina. Angela, this is Bonnie. One of my friends from uni."

"Hello, Bonnie."

Angela held out her hand and they shook competently, three tugs, up down and up, while they looked at each other. Belle stood between them and rocked back and forth on her heels like a jovial sergeant major.

"Bonnie's got a degree in Australian literature and philosophy."

It was touching that Belle actually remembered her majors. They'd had no classes in common and had only become friends through the Film Society.

" … but she has decided, for reasons that are unclear to her friends, to take up drumming. She sits at home every night and hits two sticks against a rubber pad."

"The creative urge," Angela said, "is not structured by class rooms, Belle."

Belle looked chastened.

"Well no, that's true I suppose."

Bonnie had never seen Belle so assenting.

"Maybe the fascination is that there aren't many women playing drums. Is that true?"

"Dunno. We're still a rare breed. But I took it up … well I don't really know why but it —"

She mumbled off into silence. Angela nodded as though Bonnie had unearthed a long hidden mystery.

"I first went to an audition because my boyfriend wanted to become an actor. I auditioned for a part as well just to keep him company."

The word boyfriend fell like a brick through the floor.

"Did he get the part?"

Bonnie sensed the ending of this.

"No."

"But you did?" Belle guessed.

"Yes. He didn't talk to me for a week."

Angela looked at Belle.

"Well, my dear …"

She's going. *Please don't go yet.*

"Thanks for the party. I'm off. I need to get some rest before Sunday."

She looked at Bonnie.

"Nice to meet you. Don't let Belle's lack of vision put you off your music."

Bonnie beamed.

"Are you working on a film at the moment?"

"No. I'm trying out TV for the first time. I'm hosting a show called *Sunday*

Live. Arts and variety show. It gives me carte blanche to interview anyone I like. We're doing the second show on Sunday."

Bonnie squeezed her beer can. It gave a loud crack.

"Live television … Can I come and watch?"

Only twice in her life had she mustered this sort of courage. Where did it come from? It came from a panic that she was about to be deserted. When someone important was about to walk out of her life. For a moment she saw Nora standing in the doorway in a dressing gown, the light behind her.

Angela looked at Bonnie. Bonnie felt the search behind it, a quick stab of inquiry that said 'are you someone I can trust?' Bonnie felt as if it had been a physical prodding into her gut. Before she could summon herself to appear worthy, Angela nodded.

"All right. If you want. It's not exactly intimate. And you'll do a lot of sitting around."

Bonnie nodded keenly as if to say 'Ah yes, great. Sitting around. Good!'

"Belle, why don't you come along too? Morgan'll be there."

Bonnie was looking down at Angela's stilettos when she smiled goodbye and swirled out the door. The party deflated suddenly.

"She smiled at me while I was staring at her bloody shoes."

"So?"

"And I cracked that beer can while she was talking to me. She almost jumped."

"You'll live."

"And I was grinding my teeth —"

"Bonnie, for someone who doesn't want a sex life —"

"I didn't say I didn't want one. Look!"

She showed Belle her arms.

" Remember you said feel it? I've got goose bumps."

"You better calm down before Sunday."

"I couldn't go! I was just making conversation."

"She'd be hurt."

"She'll forget I exist in five minutes. I bet she has already."

"Give her some credit, Bon. Just because she's famous doesn't mean she's an arrogant shit. We'll go. But I don't know why she held Morgan out as some sort of treat."

"Who's Morgan?"

"Her husband. An extremely boring man."

"What's he do?"

"Economist, accountant, something like that."

Belle had an airy disregard for earthier pursuits.

"Any kids?"

"Not that I know of. Are you all right?"

"I have to go home."

Bonnie was weak, dizzy. She was sickening for something. She was ill, feverish. She was debilitated by attraction, she told Belle. Belle said she didn't look that bad to her.

"And you haven't even met mystery woman."

"I did meet her," Bonnie said.

"It wasn't Angela."

"Yes it was. Remember? You said 'you'll know her when you see her'."

"Very funny."

Bonnie stood for a while on the front step. Angela Corbina had stood here not ten minutes ago, looking for car keys in her bag. Did she have a car? Or perhaps she'd walked up the street, the street lamp several metres away casting light on her as she waited for a taxi.

Bonnie caught a cab home and threw herself on her bed. The walls of her tiny room, covered in a wallpaper of fake wooden beams, shrank and swelled, shrank and swelled. She was not drunk but was dizzy from some strange lack of equilibrium. Joyous and explosive. Barely controllable. She took off her jeans, her shirt, her underpants. Her body had never felt so alive or so healthy. She felt ready to breed. She needed a brood of younger lesbians to pass this precious emotion on to. She lay between the bed sheets and stroked herself until she was running liquid velvet.

Hello, Bonnie, I just thought I'd come and see you. We taped the show tonight. I wished you'd been there. Golly it's hot in this room isn't it? Do you have a dimmer switch to keep the heat down?

Her mouth was freezing now.

Oh well, I'll just take my shirt off. whew! pass me your glass, you're looking thirsty. And beautiful. Come here and kiss me, feel my breasts.

Her clitoris shaped itself into a small hard kernel.

Go on, and I'll feel yours.

She was a river. No, she was molten hot lava, not cold water, and when she came she told Angela about it, as though her famous polite body was lying beneath her and her hands were kneading Bonnie's back.

Her drum kit sat in the corner, unglanced at, unplayed. Traffic flowed down Crown Street in regular sedate rows.

*

"Belle Belle Belle … " The security man flipped the page.

"Here you are. Park in visitors parking."

They drove through. Bonnie felt silly and speedy like a child on a special outing.

"Hey! Look at that Mercedes sports! You'll have one of those one day."

33

Belle considered. "No. Not what you'd call a practical vehicle."

She found a spot to nose the ute into and pulled the hand brake on and looked across at Bonnie.

"You've got your Sunday morning whale eyes. How much sleep did you get?"

"Sleep? Who slept?"

"And your hair could do with a comb through it. Have you got one?"

"No."

"Just put your jacket on then."

Bonnie was glad she had dressed in a vaguely decent way. She wore a shirt with sleeves, not a T shirt, so that the collar would lap nicely over the lapels of her leather jacket. Belle had a jacket slung over one shoulder. They walked across the car park and into what looked like an aircraft hangar with high corrugated iron ceilings and long narrow windows. There was the smell of fresh wood and paint. Sets lay at all angles and in pieces, as if they'd been dumped quickly. A dazzling white kitchen stood on a large flat loading truck.

A man was chopping vegetables efficiently on a wooden board at the sink and talking to a woman next to him. She had a clipboard in her hand and was echoing his remarks to another woman in thick make-up who stood off to one side. She nodded and looked bored. As Belle and Bonnie passed, she lifted her right foot out of its stiletto shoe and examined the stocking.

Bonnie thought about Angela's stilettos.

"She presents the morning show after Angela. There's a cooking section."

"I know, I've seen it."

They walked through two plastic doors and into a corridor. The walls seemed flimsy and ill-constructed. A make-up room was off on the right.

"Everything looks really fake."

"It is."

"And really temporary."

"It is."

The next door had two small metal slots screwed into the middle of it. A piece of white cardboard had been inserted between the metal. "ANGELA CORBINA" was spelt out in neat block print on the cardboard but this too had a temporary feel to it as though it would be taken out and replaced as soon as the show was finished. Belle and Bonnie stood at the door and looked at each other. It seemed like an important moment. A good time to hesitate. Belle knocked on the door very softly. The door was opened by a neat man with a grey beard.

"Come in come in," he said.

They did. He shut the door after them, almost hitting Bonnie in the back. The entire room measured no more than five feet by eight feet.

Angela sat facing a large mirror. She was applying something on a small

34

brush to her eyebrows. A white ledge was bolted underneath the mirror which ran the length of the wall and held a make-up bag and a small bottle of mineral water. She smiled at their reflections.

"Morgan, do you remember Belle? She worked on *Winter Dragons.*"

They shook hands.

"And this is her friend Bonnie. She's a drummer."

One eyebrow was raised. He didn't shake.

"Heavens! I didn't know women drummed!"

He emphasised the word, making it ridiculous. Bonnie felt like a little wind-up toy soldier. Red tin drum and tall black hat.

"That's exactly what I said. Poor Bonnie. You must get that all the time."

No, you didn't say that, Bonnie wanted to protest. You said something a lot more poetic about creativity and ...

"Yes, but it's fine. You would get worse, I would imagine."

Angela kept applying whatever it was to her eyebrows. Bonnie felt her cheeks grow hot.

"I mean, people saying the same thing to you all the time. The same comments."

Angela smiled.

"Yes, sometimes."

Morgan sat down on the ledge next to Angela.

"I'm going, darling."

He leaned down and kissed her carefully and quickly so that nothing that had been applied would come off.

"I'll be back soon."

She turned to Belle and Bonnie.

"Morgan's giving a paper at Sydney University. There's a conference on Post-modern Economics."

Who really cared? But he straightened up importantly and put his fingers through the handle of his briefcase. "Break a leg." He lifted it, opened the door and was gone.

The room relaxed. Bonnie plonked herself in a chair in the corner. She watched Angela cloud her face with powder. If I had a face like that, she thought, I'd leave it exactly the way it was.

Angela zipped up her plastic make-up kit and reached into a narrow wardrobe. She pulled out a white silk shirt that was finely ribbed with black stripes and held it out for inspection.

"Do you think it'll strobe?" she asked Belle. Belle gave it a professional glance.

"It may, yes."

Belle sat with her legs crossed and her hands behind her head as though she had been in and out of this room all her life.

What a ham! Bonnie thought. Only Belle would say it *may* instead of *it might*. Angela took out another shirt, more timid in pattern but in the same style.

"How about this one?"

There was a knock at the door. "Half an hour," a voice said

"Yeah, that shirt's better," Belle said. And then Angela rose from her chair and crossed her arms in front of her stomach to grab the edges of her shirt. Please no, thought Bonnie.

Angela took her shirt off.

How can she do that? How can she just do that in front of me? Angela kept talking while she undressed but Bonnie's ears were filled with the wax of embarrassment and slow insistent longing. I don't need to be tied to a mast, she thought. I can see her lips move but I can't hear a thing.

Belle chatted about the show, about television. She and Angela exchanged gossip. Bonnie didn't hear a word of that either. Was her silence very obvious? She felt a knot of pain as if someone were pressing down very spitefully on her stomach. Never had physical attraction been accompanied by pain such as this. It was not the fun that she supposed it might be. She wanted to crawl away and reduce herself to nothing.

Angela's bra was a dazzling snow-drop white. Look at me, it said, I'm cupping these beautiful breasts. Go on, look! Bonnie closed her eyes. *I'll move to a small town, get a job in a little library somewhere and I'll stamp books all day.* She forgot to breathe.

She opened her eyes when she realised the talk had trailed off. Angela was watching her with a small frown of concern. Bonnie's face flamed and she dropped her eyes to the white laminex dresser. Belle was examining a spot on the wall. Outside, the nasal-voiced PA system called someone to reception.

"Are you all right?" Angela asked. "You look a bit hot."

"I think the air conditioning's a bit warm."

Angela picked up the mineral water bottle.

"Drink some of this. It's cold."

She watched Bonnie take it, tilt it and drink. She didn't stop watching until Bonnie had put the bottle back on the dresser and brushed vaguely at her lips. Then she turned and reached into the wardrobe to hang her old shirt up. Muscles moved below her skin. She lifted the new shirt over her head. Silk floated for long seconds before landing parachute-like onto her shoulders and the tips of her breasts, as if it were claiming them after a long absence. Then she stood. Belle was prodding Bonnie.

"Bonnie, you coming?"

The three of them marched down the corridor. Angela's shoes went toc toc toc on the floor. People in the corridor greeted her as they went about

36

their business. Belle and Bonnie fell back like a couple of uncertain ducklings.

"Hi, Mrs Corbina."

"Hi Angela."

"Good to see you here."

"Show went well last week."

"Good luck today."

She said hello again and again, her cue cards held between the thumb and first finger of her right hand. At one point she turned to Bonnie and said in a low voice "Must be a slow day here. Last week the place was crawling with big stars. I didn't get a second glance."

She was smiling, enjoying the irony of it; at the same time including Bonnie as a streetwise co-conspirator in the long-running joke that was show business. They reached a large sliding door marked Studio A.

"Here goes," Angela said.

She opened the door and they adjusted their eyes to the darkness. People grabbed her. They touched her, dabbed at her face with a small sponge, clipped a radio mike onto her shirt and gave urgent rushed instructions as if to say 'Where the hell've you been? Oh well you're here now so listen carefully'.

Angela nodded again and again, was given a glass of water and moved further into the studio until she was standing on the edge of the set itself. There was an emergency. Some guest hadn't arrived yet. He was in the second segment so there'd have to be some reshuffling. Hands were on her back, pushing politely. They owned her.

Belle was chatting to one of the stage hands. She always found someone to talk to. Bonnie would stand in a corner and watch, talking to no-one. Belle always had names and phone numbers by the end of the night. Bonnie looked for a dark spot to stand in. In a studio there were plenty.

She became aware of a babble of noise above her head and looked up. People sat in rows of wooden seats — like circus seats — gazing around excitedly in the dark, looking at the set. When they saw Angela standing half in half out of the light, the talking grew more focussed.

"She looks thinner in real life," a man said.

"Television always makes people look wider."

"Those shoes are a bit crummy."

"People at home won't see them so it doesn't matter."

"But we're here," the first man said.

"We don't matter though," the woman said comfortably. It was true. In the greater scheme of things, in the grand sweep of electronic media, these people were so many ants brought in for atmosphere. The man insisted again that she could have taken more trouble.

A countdown blasted in loud insistent beeps. The set had cleared.

Angela was positioned behind a desk. She sat with her head down.

Theme music started up and on the monitor above her head Bonnie saw Angela lift her head as though someone had tugged a string. She smiled.

"Good morning and welcome to *Sunday Live.*" A stagy version of her real voice. A semi-circle of what Bonnie supposed were the producer, co-producer and assorted researchers stood at the side of the set. A floor manager prowled. Camera men whirled their machines around the studio like silent dance partners. They had their moves mapped out for them on clipboards.

"Timothy Carroll will also be our guest today."

She read well from the autocue. A woman at the far end of the studio fed a long strip of paper through the machine. If the words flowed through too quickly or too slowly, Angela would look inept and bumbling. The woman had to listen and watch constantly. From different ends of the studio they danced together in an electronic two step — pausing together for Angela's breath, speeding up for an emphasis, now rushing to the next topic with a slight lift of tone.

" ... talk about his new film *Body Coins.* Timothy!"

Angela swivelled around and smiled at the darkness next to her. The lights came up so suddenly from black that Timothy blinked.

"Hi Angela."

"Thanks for joining us. There's a rumour going around that this new film could be the one that will do it for you."

Do it for you? Bonnie exchanged a look with Belle. She listened to the interview for a while. There was a lot of shifting up in the circus seats. People were whispering. During the first commercial break Angela stayed at her desk. It was the floor manager who walked around, charming the circus audience and urging them to clap louder in the next segment.

"Can I go up and talk to her?" a woman in the first row asked.

The floor manager led her across the floor and up onto the set. Angela shook her hand and chatted to her. The woman scooted back to her seat, flushed.

'Well?" her husband asked.

"She's lovely! Really lovely."

Bonnie found Belle.

"I'm going outside for a while."

She sat on a bench in the corridor. She heard the countdown into the next segment and Angela's intimate welcome back that sounded like purring. It would have been good to have her drumsticks. She tapped both her middle fingers on the seats either side of her.

Left right left left, right left right right.

She stayed in the corridor listening to the flow and exchange of voices. She heard the loud artificial dialogue from a film and the audience's polite applause. She should be at home practising for the opening night of *Naked City*, not sitting here where she didn't belong. Thinking about opening night made her chest lurch. She slid her hand under her shirt. Her heart was beating in little skips. Maybe she should see a doctor. Could a drummer have arrhythmia? Belle came out and sat down.

"Aren't you coming back in?"

Left … left … right … right.

"No."

"You all right?"

"No."

"Do you want to go then? Have coffee somewhere?"

"Yes, please."

Bonnie had become a trauma patient.

"She's so self-contained!"

"She's working, Bon. It's not a dinner party."

She doesn't need me! Bonnie wanted to wail. I want to be needed by her!

"I'll just tell her we're leaving."

Bonnie stayed slumped on the bench. There was a moral here, if she could find it. Her own naiveté astounded her. She had been playing a game with a woman who was spinning around in another galaxy. She and Belle walked back to the car park.

"I know how you feel. When you want someone to be a lesbian so much and —"

"She doesn't even have to be a lesbian. She just has to want to sleep with me."

The security guard waved cheerily as they slid out onto the road. They drove down the Pacific Highway in silence and swung onto the Cahill Expressway. Belle tipped a cigarette out of its packet and lit it with one hand.

"Did she say anything when we left?"

"Nothing much."

But Belle's mouth twitched.

"You're hiding something."

Belle stopped, transferred the cigarette to her left hand, and threw money down the toll chute. When she turned back to Bonnie she was smiling.

"She said she was sorry you couldn't stay and —"

"You plural or you as in just me?"

"You you, not you us. And she said that she'd love to come."

Bonnie felt a flutter of dread. Followed by a flutter of hope.

"Come where?"

"To the opening night of *Naked City!*"

"Belle! You didn't ask her. Tell me you didn't't!"

"I did."

"She would have said yes just to be polite."

"No. She said yes because she was coming anyway."

"Why?"

"Her brother's in it, she said."

Bonnie felt the game start up again.

"Who is he? What's his name?"

"She didn't say. There's something else, though. I saw Morgan sitting in the green room. He was watching the show on the monitor and he had his arm around some girl."

"Why's he fondling some girl when Angela is so gorgeous?"

"Why indeed! On the way out I snuck another look. They were kissing."

This image quieted them both. Bonnie remembered the first, the only time a boy kissed her at a school dance, his arm around her like a vice. Their tongues dry and nervous. Her friends were kissing their boyfriends in the hard-backed chairs next to her. God knows they had all sat in that line of chairs for hours in the dark. Waiting for someone to tell them when. How. She had tasted the kiss without passion. It was just a transaction, like a long overdue deposit into an account. But she could hear the music and feel the puffy cotton dress she wore. Every other girl in the hall wore satin flares. She had worn the dress once. Twice, if she counted standing stiffly in front of the hallway mirror while her mother patted and pinned the hem and called out 'hold still!' She'd come home from the dance with sweat trickling down her back and the dress clinging like glad wrap. And her opinion of boys firmly formed.

The air over the harbour seemed delicate with hope and possibility.

"She was teasing you, I hope you realise," Belle said. "All that stuff about 'are you hot?' She knew you were wriggling like a worm on a hook."

"I just went along with it," Bonnie said.

"Of course."

Something clattered and bumped in the back of the ute in a little rhythm of its own.

"Hear that?" Bonnie said. "Six eight time."

"Tripods," was all Belle said. "I should stop and tie them up."

Bonnie sang along with the rattling tripods as they drove down George St, through Haymarket, up through Glebe and then she stopped singing when Belle parked the car. She looked around happily when she heard the crunch of the handbrake.

"I nicked her water bottle anyway."

"Well, that settles it. Now you're soul mates."

*

On the morning of opening night, Fourwords hoisted the *Naked City* sign up onto the roof. He tested the string of lights that hung across the entrance. He worked in an absorbed silence on the roof, looking up at the sky every now and then. Clouds were gathering.

In the afternoon, the cast arrived for last minute notes.

"I hope we all slept well?" Simon said.

A light wind was rattling the roof. If it rained during the play the cast would have to shout to be heard. James, his voice still strained and hoarse, looked anxious. Bonnie sat at her drum kit and tuned each tom, gently tapping and adjusting. She knew enough to occupy her hands. Her stomach knotted and clenched with anxiety.

The cast was a mess of nerves. There were flareups of temper. Billy threw a cup at someone. Simon's voice was a whisper by four o'clock. James did vocal warmups, first quietly and then loudly, going up and down the scales until he was told to shove his fucking opera queen act.

Empty cigarette packs everywhere. Half-eaten bags of lozenges. There was silence at last, while actors picked at food or slept in corners. Fourwords cleaned the stage with robotic sweeps of a broom. Bonnie went out into the foyer and looked at the guest list. There was her mother and Belle. She scanned the names and saw Angela Corbina right at the bottom. There was a question mark next to it in red biro. What did that mean? That she wasn't coming? She prayed to any small gods that may be listening for the non-appearance of Angela Corbina.

Fourwords came out and saw her with the list in her hand. He scowled.

"Doors open in five minutes."

Even now her mother and Belle might be standing outside waiting for the doors to open. "I said to her is it a career?" Clara re-exploring a favoured topic. "Can you make money from it?" Bonnie imagined Belle nodding sagely. "Exactly! I said to her once when are you going to go out and make a bit of money from all this?" "Oh well. As long as she enjoys it." And then Nora and Melanie would arrive and Nora would give her a mother a kiss and talk about clowning.

Bonnie sat in the dressing room and burred her sticks against a practice pad. Naked men muttered and swore around her. Her stomach bubbled and churned. Simon gripped her shoulders and gave her reflection a cheery grin.

"Scenes two, five and seven. Are you ready?"

"No."

"Full house out there."

His eyes glittered and the sound of him rubbing his hands as he paced back and forth sandpapered her nerves.

She stood backstage holding her sticks and listened. The emotional wrecks of five minutes ago were actually acting the opening scene. The script, energised by nerves, had come alive. There was a gasp from the audience as the body was discovered. James was suddenly next to her.

"That's no body, that's my wife," he whispered. He was buoyant with the energy that was on stage. He was trembling with it.

They waited for their cue and it came, muffled through the backdrop.

"Someone must tell him."

Actors left the stage quickly, leaving a tang of nervous sweat. Fourwords sat motionless on a stool with the script in his hand and pointed a finger at them. Bonnie walked out from a deserted, closed-in darkness into an inhabited, endless one. A random thread of light lit up her drum stool. As clear as a bell she heard her mother say "there she is" and then Bonnie was sitting behind the kit. Out of the transparent drum heads came the reflection of her own anxious face. The Indian beat started up out of her hands. The red light came up slowly.

The drums changed everything.

James circled the stage, his face transformed into a mask of agony. His head went back.

"Augh!"

They were together on every beat. His voice floated up above the audience with the drums — not drowned out by them. Her body had detached itself. Her hands and feet performed without her. She scaled up the rock face so easily. She was not thinking. Unaware of her hands but knowing the paths they travelled. Good. Don't have thoughts. Just climb the rhythm to the top. The end was coming. Shoulders down.

There!

The body was over James' shoulder and he exited slowly, mournfully. The red light faded and she stumbled offstage. James was waiting for her in the dressing room. His eyes were manic, glinting!

"We were superb, my dear, sue-*perb*."

He danced around, whipping a towel at himself and her. His penis bounced around as if it were caught up in the merriment. Time had raced out there, Bonnie marvelled. A five minute scene had become a mere moment.

"You look so serious when you play! My wife died, not yours. And whoever that is, tell them not to shriek every time you make an appearance. My God," he rolled his eyes, "talk about being upstaged. Who have you got out there anyway?"

Out there. Her mother, Melanie, Nora and Belle. Little orbiting satellites. She opened her mouth to tell him and to ask him in turn but he stood frozen, listening to the speaker on the wall.

"My cue!" and he was gone.

Bonnie sat in the long, mirrored dressing room full of socks and clothes and nervous sweat. She leaned forward and wrote

Angela

Angela

Angela

on the dressing room mirror with a finger. It cut through the grease on the glass. She would talk to Angela in the foyer. She smiled at her own image that was doubling doubling until it disappeared into a gallery of selves.

*

The audience roared warmth and approval. Six naked men and Bonnie in her black clothes, somehow more visible than the others, linked hands and bowed. Among the sea of little faces bobbed her mother and Belle, Melanie and Nora. Bonnie's facial muscles froze in a stupid grin. James squeezed her hand and they bowed again.

The foyer was full of the audience, broken free and out of their seats rushing in a wave to the free cheese and wine. Nora and Melanie found Bonnie first. Melanie wore a spangly cheese-cloth shirt. Nora wore a knitted black beanie with the word, Jessie, embroidered in gold thread along the side.

"Hey, big star." While Nora hugged her Bonnie searched the room over her shoulder. The place was wall to wall people. Everyone was shouting.

"You were fantastic!" Melanie said. "Those drums really echoed through the place. Weird seeing those dicks dangling everywhere."

"Photo time!"

Nora took a step back, forcing a path into the crowd, and lifted her Nikon. Melanie and Bonnie grinned at the lens. There was a sort of half click.

"Sorry!" Nora yelled. "Have to wait for the flash."

Melanie groaned.

When Bonnie looked at the photo later she saw herself still clutching her drumsticks with a distracted smile. The flash gave her eyes a feral look. Melanie had an arm round her shoulder and her eyes were crinkled against the smoke. The small mirrors in her shirt glittered.

And now Belle and Clara approached with cups and a plate. Belle wore a long silk cape that flowed around her shoulders and arms.

"I can't find my cigarettes with this on. No pockets."

'This wine is awful," was the first thing her mother said.

"Don't fall for that," said Belle. "Your mother cried for the entire second scene."

She winked at both Melanie and Nora but Bonnie sensed the flick of lashes was pointed more at Nora. She suspected that Nora could easily stray in Belle's direction.

"Well, I must say the hours of practice have paid off. But you look so serious when you play!" Clara squeezed her daughter's shoulder and then fingered the cloth of her T shirt. "I can see why you have to wear black but why don't you wear something a bit more ... not tattered?"

"Ma, you just paid me a compliment. Don't spoil it."

Melanie lifted her cup.

"Anyway. To music."

"Yes. May a living be made from it one day," said her mother.

"Hear hear!" said Belle.

"To art, not money!" Bonnie said.

Nora held up one of Bonnie's arms and forced it into a right angle. "Look at these muscles she's getting!"

Bonnie flexed her biceps.

"She's always been like that. Even in primary school kids said 'show us your muscles, Bonnie!' and she did, every time."

Bonnie threw her other arm behind her and crouched into full body building position.

"She'll be oiling them soon," Belle said.

And then Bonnie saw Angela. She was near the door, nodding to someone whose face she couldn't see. Maybe the neat husband had deigned to be dragged along. Light rendered her skin incandescent. While Bonnie stood frozen in her body building pose Angela stood breathing the same air, struggling against the same push of people, trying not to look tall and famous. *Please! Don't look around.* But Angela looked before she could straighten up. Their eyes met and Angela's brows arched in some sort of question. Then she smiled. Bonnie straightened, released from the spell.

"I have to go somewhere. Back in a tick."

She pushed past people, scraping someone's bare back with her sticks so that she had to stop and apologise. When she looked ahead to get her bearings, Angela had disappeared.

Simon gripped her hand.

"You were good tonight."

"Thanks."

"Notes tomorrow at three o'clock. Five o'clock show, don't forget."

And then she saw that Angela had walked over and was being introduced to her mother and Nora. Thank God for Belle, who turned around smoothly to take Bonnie's arm.

"Ah, Bonnie. Angela's here. I've just introduced everyone."

"Hi Bonnie. Great playing."

"Thank you."

There was a small tight silence. Clara cleared her throat and looked at the well-known actress.

44

"So how long have you known my daughter?"

Bonnie lowered her head as if commencing prayer. Angela looked startled but her voice didn't show it.

"This is the third time we've met. Is it, Bonnie?"

Bonnie nodded, her eyes still lowered. Sweat beaded down her back.

"You know about these things," Clara said. She tossed her head back and looked Angela in the eye. "Do you think she has potential as a drummer?"

"Ah." Angela scraped a hand through her hair. "Well. I don't know much about music. She has a feel for it. She had no score, did you Bonnie? No, and I think improvising is always hard. And she was all there was in terms of atmosphere really. There was no-one else up there."

Bonnie loved her with an ache. Another silence. Even Belle was speechless.

"It's interesting, the whole question of art and vocation. I must say when it comes to improvisation I prefer clowning to serious theatre," said Nora. "There's an art to clowning."

"Clowning?" Angela said.

"So you think she'll be all right?" Clara asked.

"Who?"

"Bonnie."

"Of course." Angela looked over at Belle who gave her a broad reassuring smile. She wants confirmation that we're sane, Bonnie thought grimly.

Nora tried again. "It's come a bit late in life but I've found it through these workshops."

"Found what?" Angela asked. Her tone was now edged with steel. Maybe she felt she was being made a fool of. She and Nora were shifting positions. Animosity had changed their expressions. Both of them folded their arms without even realising it.

"My inner clown. But I'd have to say tumble turns are the hardest thing I've ever done."

"Really."

"Nora used to be Bonnie's English teacher," Clara told Angela.

This news interested Angela more. She looked from Nora to Bonnie and back again. Bonnie thought this is what hell must be like. Public humiliation, unwanted disclosures, a place where you want to sink into the ground over and over, except you can't. And hell would have no music. And then the mood changed. Angela unfolded her arms and reached over to shake Clara's hand. "Well it's been nice to meet you all but I really have to go. It looks like rain."

"We do an hour of get-to-know-the-group and then we split into three teams."

"Bye Bonnie."

Angela travelled across the room and took Morgan by the arm.

"It's just a matter of time. At first I wouldn't let myself bend but …"

"Nora, shut up. She's gone."

Clara looked wistful. "I must say she's very elegant."

"What rain did she mean?" Nora said. "It's not raining."

"It was an excuse," Bonnie said. "You were boring her to death."

"It's the Nora Driver test of friendship," Melanie said. "If they can be interested in clowning for five minutes they're in."

"She's not very friendly," Nora said.

"Look," Clara said. "She's had to do a circuit of the room like royalty. Everyone's watching. Imagine what that feels like!"

"She hates it," Bonnie said.

"How do you know?" asked Nora.

"Now she's at the door," Clara told them, as if they were all blindfolded. She gave Angela a wave. But Angela didn't wave back. She and Morgan disappeared. There was a great roar as if a gigantic flock of birds was suddenly beating their wings against everyone's ears. People looked up at the ceiling, wineglasses in their hands. The noise grew louder.

"Jesus Christ!" shouted Melanie "It's rain!"

The deluge had started.

"Mum, why did you tell her about Nora being my teacher?"

But Clara didn't hear the question.

"Did you notice," she whispered, "that she only shook my hand?"

*

Nora rang the next day.

"All right," she said "tell me."

"Tell you what?"

"Have you got the hots for this woman?"

"Which woman?"

"That famous woman from last night. Mrs She Has A Feel For It!"

"You were acting very strange last night."

"So do you?"

"You were embarrassing me."

"No I wasn't. She's just pretentious. So, have you got the hots for her?"

"She's married."

"Why was she there last night anyway?"

"Her brother's in the show."

"What's he like?"

"I don't know who he is."

'You don't know?"

"I can't be too obsessed if I haven't found out."

"Good. Stick to your drumming."

"Can't I have a sex life? Why do you get all the fun?"

"Famous people chew you up and spit you out. Let me tell you a cautionary tale."

"I have to go."

"Well, if you need me just ring. Melanie says hi."

"OK."

The Wastelandish looked hungover and worn. The foyer floor had been swept but bits of cheese and empty cups were scattered over the counter. Fourwords sat a wettex at one end and shaped it into a high blue tide that swept cheese and jatz crumbs into a bucket. He looked at her, his face blank.

Simon sat whistling some show tune. His feet tapped and bounced on the concrete. James came in and kissed her on the cheek. He smelled of mint toothpaste and shampoo. His hair glistened wet.

"Hey, James have you got a sister?"

"No. Job's yours if you want it."

Fourwords dropped the wettex in the bucket with a loud splash. James winked at her and disappeared out the back.

So it wasn't James. She sat in the auditorium with the cast and listened to Simon's critique of their first night. She examined them for clues. None of them looked anything like Angela. Was it Billy? He sat frowning with concentration next to his boyfriend. They leaned together like two campfire sticks and sex hung in the space around them like thick vapour. Bonnie tried to see them fucking hot and close, their faces red and blinded, but the image wouldn't come.

Rain started pelting the tin roof again, drowning out Simon's voice. Everyone groaned. Even dedicated Wastelandish followers would stay at home on a day like this. It was the beginning of winter, the worst theatre season. Bonnie didn't care as long as she was playing.

Someone tapped her on the shoulder. It was Fourwords bending down and breathing an inch from her cheek. She could smell the turpentine on his skin.

"Can I talk to you?"

He led her into the dressing room and sat her down at a chair.

"Did you write that?"

Bonnie made out the words on the mirror.

Angela

Angela

Angela

They were more crooked than she remembered but they had survived the night. So had all the reflections of her selves, which looked at Fourwords defiantly.

"Yep."

"Why?"

"Is she *your* sister then?"

"Yep. She's married."

It was unbelievable that they were related. Fourwords' body was without beauty or mystery. Where Angela's thoughts radiated light and moved her face to form words or laughter, his face was sunk in a permanent blank. He looked at Bonnie.

"She's married, I said."

"Christ, I know she's married! Can't I admire the woman without everyone getting into a tizz?"

Bonnie leaned over and smeared the letters away with her sleeve. Thunder cracked above the tin roof. Everything rattled.

"Hear that? That's God saying 'leave those words on that mirror'."

"Everyone wants a piece of her. She doesn't need some kid mooning and moping over her."

A long speech for Fourwords.

"I was not mooning and moping."

"She's not a fucking dyke, OK? Forget it. Run after someone else."

He slammed out and left the air thick with anger and unspoken threat. That afternoon her sticks turned into two limp strands when she played and her timing fell everywhere. Fourwords sat in his dark corner with the script and a torch. He didn't look at her but his presence made her waver and fumble. He had made her feel like garbage. And garbage plays badly. She felt off balance. Nothing was easy. Nothing flowed. James' scene was weak and ineffectual. He had to shout above the rain on the roof.

In the dressing room she threw socks at the ceiling and hoped it would rain louder so that her faltering pitter patterings would be drowned out. She threw her dream of Angela away. No more fantasies. From now on, nothing but the real world.

*

Her mother rang.

"Isn't this rain fantastic? I've got a surprise for you. Come on over."

Her mother opened the door and skipped up the hall. Bonnie trailed behind her, feeling old. There was a smell of coffee.

"Ta da!"

A large round nylon bag dangled from Clara's hand.

"What is it?"

"It's a bag for those cymbals of yours! Haven't you seen one before?"

"Is it my birthday or something?" Her mother didn't give out presents willy nilly.

"Can't I give my daughter something once in a while?"

Bonnie sat at the table and propped her head on her hands.

"What's up?"

"I don't know. Life."

"Is that all."

"Do you miss having sex?" Bonnie asked her mother.

"Good God. What a question!" Her mother also sat. "Yes I do. As a matter of fact I do."

She was embarrassed enough to sound defiant. Her chair harrumphed on the wooden floor as she pulled it closer to the table.

"Not that sex with your father was all that great. But I miss the closeness, the everydayness of another body in the bed."

She glanced at a pack of cards that sat near her, tempting her to lay them out in neat rows. But she put both hands flat on the table as if to show her willingness to attend this session without distractions. Bonnie nodded and opened her mouth but her mother said quickly: "Do you miss sex with Nora?"

Bonnie swallowed.

" … aah, yes, but … it really …"

Her mother got up and brought a second cup back to the table.

"You'll have to wait for the cheese cake to thaw."

Bonnie curled her fingers around her cup and stared into the steam. Her mother sat and waited.

"I feel like I'm not going to find anyone else. Do you feel like that?"

"You know, Bonnie, when I was coming out to Australia I fell in love with a woman on the boat."

" …"

"An English woman who was coming out here to meet up with her husband just like I was. Well, I say in love but I don't know … I think it was lust. Lust," her mother repeated as if tasting it. "We got into bed together but as soon as she put her arms around me I jumped out of bed again and got dressed. I practically ran back to my cabin."

"What were you scared of?"

Clara reached out for the cards and picked them up.

"Do you know where she is now?"

"Bonnie, this was twenty five years ago. I haven't the faintest idea."

Her mother fanned through the cards briskly, making a small breeze.

"But I do remember she used to love wearing little straw hats."

"Straw hats?"

"You have to practise sex, I know that much. Not that I get much chance. And you! You're always falling in love with the wrong people. Between the —"

"I'm not!"

"Not wrong, but out of your reach. You know what I mean. But if you're worried that you'll never sleep with anyone again, don't be."

"Easy to say."

"Just don't look too hard."

"I think it's too late," Bonnie said "I think my desperation has engulfed the city."

"Then be desperate about someone else, darling. Someone real, not this actress."

Real? The woman on the boat was a bit too real, Bonnie thought. She imagined her mother kissing a woman in a hat while the ocean rocked dangerously.

"I think Angela likes me."

Her mother ran a knife through the cheesecake to see if was still frozen. She put the knife down then picked it up again and traced the tablecloth pattern with the blade.

"She's married. She's a lot older."

"Nora was older."

"Exactly," her mother said. "And look what happened. All right. It's time." Clara picked up her fork.

Bonnie and her mother devoured the cheese cake even though it hadn't completely thawed.

*

Charlie stared at her hands.

"Come on, let's hear those accents."

Triplets with an accent on the first beat. 123123123

"Don't hit the other two so hard. Then you don't have to work to get the accent to stand out."

123123123

"Better. How's the play going?'

"It finishes this weekend."

Her shoulders hurt.

"Take a break. Loosen your shoulders. What'll you do then?"

She shrugged her shoulders back and forth.

"I don't know. Find a band maybe."

After her lesson she scanned the ads on the wall of the music shop. Some bands were organised and had typed their ad neatly and photocopied their phone numbers along serrated lines so that you could tear it off easily. Some ads were just tiny scraps of paper – words scrawled on anything handy. A last minute scrabble to think up something appropriate.

'Wanted. Experienced drummer with good feel for heavy rock. Must be into Black Sabbath and other metal.' The spelling was often last minute as well. 'Good look and attitude esenttial. Own transport. Ring Allan.'

All the advertisements said 'Own transport.' or in one case 'Oun car!!!' She imagined the phone call. "I don't care how you play, man. Long as you got a car. You've got a van? Shit man, you're in." No band wanted to help the drummer lug. She didn't ring any of the numbers, although one or two appealed. She had to get a car. Own car.

On Saturday Simon gathered the cast together, naked and shivering, in the dressing room.

"OK, it's our last night. Party at my place afterwards. The address is on the notice board. No throwing up, no shooting up and for now, no fucking up. Break a leg, children. There's a big crowd out there. Enjoy, enjoy, enjoy. You've been terrific."

After Scene One she looked through the peep hole. There were no vacant seats that she could see. Two empty up the back. No, a whole row empty and then two empty seats in front.

"Good eh?" Simon said, peering next to her. "Makes you want to buy shares in the company. Coming to the party?"

"Yeah."

Belle had said she'd come tonight.

"I like wrap parties," she'd said.

"Trust you to know the term."

"They're an occasion."

Sitting backstage, Bonnie started to think about the love scene. In this scene Billy and James wore shorts. "I don't trust you two otherwise," Simon had said.

It was the part of the play when the audience went very very quiet. When James kissed Billy she could hear seats creak. Bonnie had found this scene difficult to build on. She'd tried different drums and cymbals, different sticks, various felt mallets.

"Xylophone?" Simon had suggested, but it hadn't sounded right. It needed something but the nature of that something eluded both of them. Then two weeks into the season she discovered two small finger bells that chimed softly and rang for long seconds. She also brought in a large bamboo xylophone Charlie had lent her. The combination worked. It didn't shatter the silence and it increased the tension onstage. She was happy.

Tonight, the audience were giggly and energetic. They took a while to settle. The volume dropped when James kissed Billy and when they lay on the bare floorboards together there was silence coming down from everywhere. They had their backs to the audience. It was up to Bonnie to break the silence, or enhance it. Feel it, feel it, she told herself. Wait for the moment when the quiet goes dead. The bells started tinging delicately between her thumb and first finger.

She looked to the two men to get a sense of the rhythm. Ting ... ting ... ting ... They were still kissing. Very passionately. Trust James to – but now Billy was climbing onto James. He ran a hand through his hair. James seemed to be whispering into Billy's ear. Billy lay next to James again, pressing against his back. For three seconds she bent down to pick up the mallets and shift her stool closer to the xylophone. When she looked back towards the stage the mallets nearly fell with an unholy clatter from her hand. Billy's hand was snaking its way under the elastic right down into James shorts. She could see the shape of James' erection and the lump that was Billy's knuckles closing around it moving very slowly up, down, up and then down. She started to strike the bamboo bars. The mallets jumped across and down. She did not look back at the stage till the lights were dimming and she could hearing a flat being dragged backstage by Fourwords. He was clearly not a man to be deterred by live sex on stage. She stopped playing and sat waiting for the complete dark to swallow her. How could they do it? Just have sex like that? She had seen them writhe from the corner of her eyes as she played in wooden embarrassment without subtlety or colour. Free and easy fucking. Relaxed fucking. She felt aroused by it, by their surreptitious thrusting. The light faded. She slipped off her drum stool.

"What the fuck were you two doing out there?"

Simon was raging in a half whisper. Billy and James stood grinning like kids and shivering with cold.

Bonnie wanted to ask them how it was so easy. She wanted to ask them did you have sex with each other before? Did Billy's boyfriend know? But Simon stood there blocking her way, glaring. In the dark his face glowed as white as his hair.

"No-one saw us," Billy said. But he looked unsure.

"I fucking well saw you! That's enough. If this wasn't closing night I'd —"

"That's why we did it."

"It was just a joke. We didn't come or anything," James said. "Well, I didn't. Did you, Billy?"

"Not me. I've had better sex with chairs."

"I don't care if you fuck each other till the cows come home but not during a performance."

Simon noticed Bonnie hovering.

"Oh fuck it, one more scene and then you're out of my hair."

He waved them away. James put his arms around Bonnie and Billy. They walked to the dressing room.

"Take no notice kidlets. He's on edge because Mrs Corbina's in tonight."

"Who?"

"Ugly Fourword's beautiful big sister. Simon wants to make a good impression."

He looked down at Bonnie.

"Our drummer here would like to make an impression on her too."

Bonnie went cold. Billy whistled. "Now there's a challenge."

"Bonnie's in spasms over her. Wrote her name all over the mirror."

"How do you know?"

"I heard Fourwords telling you off, the little prick."

He listened to the speaker for a second.

"Final scene in a minute." He put down the cigarette he'd been about to light. "Fourwords is an arsehole. He's a homophobic little shit. I've worked with him here before, back when he wanted to act. He's hung around the Wastelandish for years because he's talentless. His sister got all the brains." He smiled at Bonnie angelically. "I wish you could bump pussies with her just to piss him off."

Bonnie didn't mention that she'd given up her fantasy. But she leaned forward with a question.

"How are you so casual about sex? Is it just like a game for you?"

Billy and James looked at each other. There was a little surprised silence. What prim little questions! What she meant to say hadn't come out at all.

That's what happens when you're not honest, Bonnie told herself. You really wanted to ask James 'how do you come with someone? How do you let that thing inside you go with a complete stranger? With anyone?'

"When I was in kindergarten I used to kiss boys for buttons," James said. "I'd kiss them and they'd give me a button. The kindy teacher told my parents and they took me to one side and said 'James, boys don't kiss boys, they kiss girls. And when you're in kindergarten you don't kiss anyone'."

From the speaker they heard the stage cue for the scene to end. They all jumped as if bitten. As they hurried back, Bonnie said:

"They can't bring up the lights till I start."

She slipped back onto her stool. Fourwords was glaring from his corner. Billy patted him on the head just as the red light came up. She focussed on the kit in front of her. She played the pattern she always used for this scene — something she couldn't have read from a chart but which had come out of some place in her body. She ignored the black space ahead which was never quite dark enough for her to not distinguish the odd face. She forgot the six men acting out the fight scene in this strange obscure play. She didn't have to watch them; they followed her tempo. She was sitting on an island. And all around her was a multi-layered wash of rhythm and red light. She played as though driven.

The blackout washed over her. She had stopped playing. She sat and felt the skips of her heart again. Then all of a sudden James was pulling her by the hand up and out onto the centre of the stage for their last bow and saying out of the corner of his mouth, "There she is. Third row. Middle."

The worst thing was that she dropped her sticks.

4

Bonnie broke the kit apart. She lifted the toms off their mounts. She slid the legs out of the floor tom. People were flipping their seats, talking loudly as though released from a long silence. They filed out through the exits but a small knot of people stood in the far aisle. She unscrewed the wingnuts from the cymbal stands and lifted the cymbals off gently. They shone and winked in the light like huge brass hats. She spun the wingnuts carefully back onto their threads. She squatted and unclipped the kick pedal from the bass drum. The snare drum fitted snugly in its case. She stowed the cymbals into their bag.

Everything had a place. Inanimate objects were privileged in that way. They all had a place to be at any one time. It was only humans who roamed and regrouped and fantasised.

The group of people thinned. Where was Belle? She was supposed to be driving Bonnie to the party. She heard footsteps on the stage. Toc, toc, toc. Stilettos. The feet stopped in front of her.

"Hello."

She looked up. Angela in a suit, on her own, wanting an audience with Bonnie. She lowered her expensive suit onto the drum stool and watched Bonnie pack. The stool was adjusted low to the ground so that Bonnie's short legs could straddle it. Angela's knees were near her chin.

"Interesting change in that love scene, I noticed."

Bonnie went red.

"It's good to come back at the end of run and see what's changed. I don't want to sound patronising but your drumming has improved."

Angela fished something out a pocket with her right hand, glanced around the empty theatre, then bent down and put it onto the floor.

"These are Belle's car keys. She's at the party. She'll see you there, she said." She gave Bonnie a quick smile, as if she'd just remembered that she had to and then turned and disappeared into the auditorium. The keys winked on the floor boards.

All right Belle, Bonnie thought, what's going on?

In primary school she found the world a challenge to focus on. At school she went into a trance-like state when things got too hard. 'Bonnie's asleep, Miss' kids used to say. 'She's asleep with her eyes open.' Her friends nudged her awake to answer questions and she would snap back into focus. She felt like that now. Something momentous was happening but, like a tourist listening to a faroff carnival, she had no map to find where it was.

James helped her bring the drums out to Belle's ute where it squatted in the back lane. The cold night air hit the sweat patches under her arms. Maybe she'd have a shower before she went to Simon's. She could have a quick bath and think about the Angela incident.

"Everyone's taken it the wrong way," James said mournfully. "It was supposed to be funny but it came out as tasteless."

Bonnie concentrated on unlocking the canopy of the ute.

"So did you talk to her Royal Fullness?"

Bonnie hesitated.

"Not really."

"Never mind."

He threw an arm around her for a second and then walked back across the road. Bonnie walked around to the driver's door and opened it. She sat down and sighed. She had to roll the seat forward so that her feet reached the pedals. The whole world had longer legs than her. She sniffed the keys to see if they smelt of Angela.

"He's very fond of you, I can tell."

Bonnie dropped the keys into her lap in fright. Angela sat in the passenger seat. She had risen up out of nowhere like a visitation. Bonnie's heart started up its familiar flutter at a speed that frightened her. She fumbled for the keys. She felt embarrassment, excitement and a small curl of anger.

"Jesus you scared me."

"I'm sorry."

"Were you lying on the floor?"

"I didn't mean this to be so melodramatic. I'll tell you while we drive."

Angela found the keys between Bonnie's legs and handed them over. The ute roared off, barrelled down the lane and then turned right. In the back, drum cases turned and rolled.

"OK, we're driving."

"I was sitting on the floor. It was too filthy to actually lie on it."

She placed the right word in the sentence with a good deal of contentment. *Sitting* on the floor. Not lying on it.

"I didn't want people to know I was there."

Angela took up a lot of space in the cabin of the ute. She loomed. She had a large presence and it wasn't just her height, which caused her head to bump against the roof. Was it her fame? Of course it was. It sat next to her like an invisible twin. Bonnie glanced sideways at her while she drove. At her recent haircut. Her nape was exposed. Her dark brown hair was tamed in a half circle above her ears. An earring glittered.

But they were details easily dreamed and it seems to me, Bonnie thought, that I am dreaming all this. She was about to ask about *Sunday Live,* which she never watched because it reminded her of that day she sat tapping hopelessly, when Angela said:

"I had a fight with my brother about you. He's always warding people off me. He told me about what you did. I kept thinking about you writing my name on the mirror."

Bonnie could have laughed out loud except her throat was full of soft cotton.

"And then I couldn't get your face out of my mind."

Bonnie pulled the car over and stopped under a large fig tree. She switched off the engine and looked out at the street. Her map was gone. Blown out the window. She was in a car somewhere in Surry Hills, opposite the dun-coloured bricks of a day care centre and the woman next to her was so attractive that Bonnie's blood had drained permanently to her crotch. From the tree above them came the chirruping of bats. The air was the coldest she had ever felt against her skin. They would freeze sitting in this car. They would be found by small children as they came running out for a morning of innocent play. Two ice statues in a game reserve waiting for the animal to come out of hiding.

Bonnie didn't know where to drive to. She was stuck until a decision was made.

"Do you want to go to the party?"

"Don't you have to go? Aren't you guest of honour something?"

"Yes."

"Why?"

"Wastelandish was where I first acted."

Angela leaned over and kissed her. A gentle warm-lipped kiss. No fuss, no fanfare. Bonnie realised she'd been sitting waiting for her to do this. The only sound was the creak of the car seat and her drums, like an absorbed audience, shifting ever so quietly in the back. Angela held Bonnie's face in her hands and ran her finger along her jawbone. Bonnie didn't breathe but she didn't faint either.

"There's going to be more rain soon. It's going to pelt down."

Angela whispered it as though it were the darkest secret she knew. As though no deeper intimacy could be shared than the knowledge of rain coming. Questions flowered in Bonnie's mind but she only asked one.

"Isn't it too cold for rain?"

She started up the car. When they'd parked outside Simon's, Angela put a hand on Bonnie's arm.

"I'll go in first."

Bonnie nodded. There was the toc toc toc of the stilettos on concrete, a knock on the door, a voice that changed pitch when its owner saw Angela. She heard Simon's speech-making voice carry clearly through the front door, across the lawn and into the car where Bonnie sat.

" ... that have done such a fine job of this script. It hasn't been easy ..."
The door shut.

Bonnie sat and breathed in and out. She started the car and circled the block twice and then drove back and parked the car, as carefully as a chauffeur, in exactly the same spot. Her stomach felt lead-lined.

"I was just wondering," she asked an invisible Angela, "are you planning to do this a lot? Should I bring a book?"

The invisible Angela looked down at her immaculate suit, shamefaced. "I'm sorry," she said. "Let's go in together, OK?"

Simon was still speaking when Bonnie walked in. He smoothed his platinum hair forward and ruffled it back in the next movement of his hand. A large square cake stood on a table in front of him. Tiny buildings were edged in icing and little candles were waiting to be lit. The room was full of people. The six cast members were scattered everywhere and variously nodded or winked at her. James mimed nodding off to sleep while Simon talked. Belle appeared in her cape and steered her into the kitchen.

"You've just missed your praise. Best woman drummer et cetera. Great feel for atmosphere blah blah. Have a drink."

She poured what looked suspiciously like Blackberry Nip into a glass.

"So what's happening?"

"Oh well, let's see ... Angela was sitting in your car. I had heart failure. We drove. We parked under a fig tree. She kissed me. She said it's going to rain soon. I said I didn't think so. That's about it."

Belle shook her head. "Fuck."

"Why did she take your car?"

"She didn't want anyone to see her. Bon, it was weird. It was like a confession."

"Confession?"

"You know ... I'd like to meet Bonnie privately, if that's OK. That's what she said. Said she wanted an anonymous environment for a while. She went on about your face or something. And writing stuff on a mirror. Right over my head. Then we did this macho car key swap."

"I thought you said she wasn't a lesbian."

"Well, I've been trying to work it out. Angela's married. Safe inference is that Angela likes blokes. But what's this? Angela likes Bonnie! So inference two, Angela likes women."

"So much for those heterosexual wrists."

Bonnie looked at Simon's fridge magnets. They were different kinds of cheese made from hard yellow plastic. Gouda, the one with the veins, Camembert. She pulled one off the fridge.

"These wouldn't fool anyone for a second."

She took an experimental nibble.

"Deduction," Belle continued, "Angela is either totally confused. Or a closet lesbian who sleeps with women secretly."

Bonnie thought about Nora. Sitting in Nora's car, sitting in Angela's car. She might spend her life sitting in older women's vehicles. It was a good argument for buying something to get around in.

"What about Morgan?"

"She just parades Morgan in public. He's a good flesh presser. Maybe they have some sort of agreement."

There were screams of laughter from the other room and the collision of plates. The cake was being cut.

"Everything points to it. Angela's not going to show her lovers to her producer and her agent and say, 'look who I'm bonking!' There are no famous out actors in Australia. Or anywhere."

"I'm sick of closeted women."

"Then stop being attracted to them," Belle said briskly. "Anyway, there are positive aspects."

"What?"

"You could take up acting. She's got brilliant contacts. She could open doors for you."

"Are you mad? I couldn't act. I don't even lie well."

"Maybe she could get you work in musicals." Belle thought for a minute, a liqueur glass catching light between her fingers. "I don't think she sings though."

Bonnie peered through the window into the dark.

"Is that Fourwords' car?"

"Go! Go!"

Bonnie started to walk out but turned around.

"I feel like a child bride."

Belle made a shooing motion. The party had swirled itself drunkenly around one corner of the lounge room where Angela stood telling some story.

"I told him, do you think I'd let that get in my way?"

It must have been the punch line because Simon's laugh rang out in an eager gush. Bonnie had to stand on her toes to see her. She thought, how will I get her out? Does she want me to get her out? She slithered between people, a little insignificant thing, and landed among the admirers.

"Did you want a lift home, Angela?" Her voice was bright and perky. Angela did a good job of pretending to consider the offer. She put her head on one side.

"Actually, I wouldn't mind."

"Angela! You can't go yet!"

Simon hovered and fussed while the buildings on his cake toppled. In front of them, Angela became suddenly frail and small. She put a hand to her forehead.

"Sorry Simon, I think I really have to. I'm getting an excruciating headache."

People stopped eating cake and watched Angela and the small woman in a torn shirt walk down the hall together. In happier circumstances a declaration of property could have been made. Something like: "She's mine now! None of you know how to treat her properly!" They were theatre people, it could get a round of applause.

They found a back door. It clicked behind them. They were in a small back garden. Was there a back gate? There was. And it was unlocked.

"It's going to rain in about eight seconds," Angela said. She was carrying her jacket. From behind her, Bonnie could see the vertebrae in her long spine. She could have reached out and press them like buttons.

"Maybe if you took your shoes off it would be easier to walk."

One.

Bonnie shut the gate and looked around. They were in a small park behind Simon's house. A path wound away in front of them, lit by a single lamp.

Two.

They walked to the edge of the main street. It was deserted. No-one stood there wanting to take Angela away. Angela reached for her hand.

Her hand was cool. Bonnie's fingers closed around it.

Three.

"Headache eh?" said Bonnie.

"Excruciating."

There was the sound of footsteps on a path, a door opening, then closing. Far off noise made the dark close in.

Four.

Was that a count in her own head or was it Angela murmuring? She was looking up at the sky. "How did you get your name?" she asked.

Five.

"When I was born the nurse said I was bonny. My mother thought it was the nurse's job to name babies. She didn't recognise the Scottish."

"Good grief."

"I think Mum was delirious from the labour. Is it like that for you all the time? People surrounding you and adoring you?"

Six.

"Yes, so I don't tend to go to many parties. But I feel obliged to the Wastelandish."

Her drums were still nestled in the back of the ute. She opened the passenger door.

Seven.

"No, I'll drive." Angela said and toc toc tocked around to the driver's side.

"Oh all right." Bonnie clumped into the passenger's seat herself.

Eight.

"Is that you counting? Or me?"

Angela held up a finger. Rain hit the car so hard that Bonnie clapped her hands to her ears. It clamoured on the metal like impatient fists. In seconds the windscreen ran with water.

"How did you know it was going to rain?"

"Ever since I was a child I've known. My ears go strange."

Angela rolled the car seat all the way back and reached down to take off her stilettos. "Could you hang on to these? I can't drive in heels."

"Drive in them? I don't know how you breathe in them."

Bonnie was thinking about practical things still. No wonder people did it. It was a good diversion from terror. The night ahead was full of it. Angela started the car.

"When are you going to get your car back?"

"I'll ring Belle eventually."

"Are you really going to drive in this rain?"

"Can I ask you something now?"

"Yes."

"Will we go to your place?"

Bonnie imagined them in her sofa bed with the fridge rumbling whirr clunk whirr six feet away. No, she was about to say. Then she remembered Morgan.

"I don't know how to ask this but don't you have a husband?"

"He's in New Zealand. My place then?"

Bonnie nodded. She felt nervous in the presence of someone who she knew must be a seasoned performer. I should warn her, thought Bonnie as the car tyres sprayed through rivulets across every street. I should warn her that I'm hopeless in bed. The rivulets grew into streams and by the time they turned into Edgecliff Road the streets were rivers. Maybe they could just talk.

Angela drove the ute into a driveway, under a dark green roller door and then stopped. She cut the motor. Rain thundered on the tin roof.

"How are you feeling?" Angela asked.

"Cold."

But it was nerves, not cold. She felt like a parcel being carefully delivered. They got out of the ute. The brick garage with its green door was the warm dry ark and outside it was dark rain and the unknown future. They were the only two people left alive on the earth. Everyone else had been washed away in a transparent wave of not mattering. Angela started out into the rain and then pulled back to wait for Bonnie who seemed to have stalled behind her.

They stood and looked at each other. Bonnie dissolved under her gaze. It was a quiet peaceful gaze, not the questioning stare she had been subjected to that asked 'are you good or bad?' Under the look she became someone wanted and wanting.

"You're so little," Angela said. Rain ran down her face and dripped unnoticed from the end of her chin. Her famous chin.

"I'm five feet four and a half. That's average height."

But she knew Angela meant something else.

"Put your arms around my neck."

She did.

She was picked up.

There was the smell of perfume and the heat of Angela's skin where Bonnie's cheek rested on a warm shoulder. There were trees and five or six white stairs that looked mossy and slippery. Thunder rolled and reverberated above their heads in the open garden sky.

It was hard to believe that people weren't hiding behind bushes waiting to pounce and take Angela away. But the bushes moved and rustled and streamed with rain, not limbs. They stood at the front door while Angela searched for keys in her coat and then they were inside.

The rain teemed to provide a cocoon around them, even indoors. Bonnie felt again that she'd captured the object of desire without a suitable struggle and had neither the grace or wit to sustain the captive's interest. Angela led Bonnie on a guided tour of the rooms but neglected to turn on more than the hall light. So pictures, paintings and rugs seemed ghostly and unreal. Every object was only a promise of itself, despite being given a long history by Angela.

Bonnie listened to Angela introduce her possessions but kept up her own internal monologue, which seemed to be her permanent state since she had taken up music. Rhythm tapped like morse code in the part of her that was usually tilted to receive signals from the outside world. She wondered why she was getting this history of furniture. She even felt the smallest wriggle of impatience.

Finally they were back at the foot of the stairs.

"Tired yet?" Angela asked, with dry humour. Bonnie heard it as "brave enough yet?" and nodded. They walked up a stairway and into a bedroom. They peeled off each other's wet clothes. Bonnie pulled off the muddied linen jacket and trousers quickly. They were as foreign as moon rocks, part of Angela's public life. Alien flora that lived and grew in a different climate. Her stockings, shredded and ruined in the feet, were foreign as well but not so excluding. Were they silk? she wondered. Anything not cotton or flannel was a mystery to her. Bonnie shed Angela's fame from her. Below the mysterious underwear was the naked woman, slim hipped, shaven armpits, unshaven at the crotch and legs. Her skin was pale and flawless, except for a spattering of freckles on her strong arms and back.

"Now me," Angela said.

Angela took delight in every piece of clothing that Bonnie wore. She unlaced her ancient blue gymboots slowly and cradled them in her hands as though they were treasures.

"Look at these," she muttered to herself "What does it say on the side? Arch Cushion Support. Isn't that fantastic?"

She removed Bonnie's jeans, working them gently down and off, and pressed them against her face. Bonnie was heavy with embarrassment and groaned into the pillow: "they're only gymboots. They're my oldest jeans!"

She smelt Bonnie's T shirt after she'd unpeeled it like a thin black fruit. If she does this to my clothes, Bonnie thought, what will she do to me?

But she didn't feel any fear. This woman was strange and lovely and gentle enough for Bonnie's desire to suddenly stop its automatic retreat and loiter with clear intent. Her nipples were sharp and keen with it. She played Angela's game of inspection, offering her clothes and body up to Angela's hands and eyes until it was Bonnie's turn and then she took the beautiful face between her hands and kissed it over and over. Turned her body over and kissed the small buttons of spine down to her bottom while a moan came up from Angela. She kissed and bit both the cheeks and made a noise at the moisture on her fingers when she dipped them slowly into the velvet of Angela's cunt. When the exploring finger moved around inside, Angela lifted her rear end off the bed.

"I have to turn you over." Bonnie whispered to her back. And she did. When she lay looking up at Bonnie, Angela spread her legs so wide in welcome and pulled Bonnie down so hard that her internal heat rose up and met the wet heat descending. And then their mouths kissed for the first time and both of them moved and moved and moved.

Bonnie did not know where the surface of her body had gone. Her skin absorbed Angela's body and released her own blood so that it raced past her ears in loud pulses. She had no choice in any movement. Just as an object falls toward earth in a pre-ordained path, there was no ambiguity. And then the explosion of reaching target.

*

A voice woke her just as she was reaching land in her dream. She was in a boat, pulling on the oars with long strokes. The boat nosed its prow onto the sand and she woke up with her face against Angela's body.

"Do you know what you look like when you play?"

"When what?"

Her body felt as soft as butter. She struggled to the surface. Angela was on her back, very neat and still, her profile pointed at the ceiling like a figurehead.

"You looked as though you were fighting yourself. Under that light I could only see your face and it was so frightened and so concentrated. It was like seeing an undiluted soul."

Bonnie held her hand out and it was caught and kissed.

"You had no body at all."

Bonnie had suspected that her body disappeared when she sat behind a drum kit. Simon said she was perfect because she vanished behind the main action onstage. She became bodiless in public.

She lifted herself onto one elbow and reached down for the sheet. Something important had just happened to her. Her body felt strangely rinsed and limp. She tucked the sheet around her chin.

"What's wrong? Are you cold?"

"No. Why did you leave so soon on opening night?"

"Morgan wanted to go."

She mentioned her husband's name as comfortably as if it was one of the pillows in the bed.

"So you're still together?"

Angela closed her eyes.

No, I won't be drawn in by her sadness, Bonnie thought. I want to know where I stand. Who he is, this bristly academic who had released the tension of the dressing room just by leaving it. What power! She had her own little spoonful of power, waiting for an answer from the actress. But the actress opened her eyes after a couple of seconds and just laughed.

"Don't worry about *him!*"

Bonnie felt she had committed some quaint social gaffe.

It could have been worse. Bonnie could have been made to sneak in through a back door and told to leave before first light. And she would have done it. He might have raged in and thrown a chair at them as they lay in the matrimonial bed.

Bonnie suddenly remembered what she had been trying to remember — that she had come with someone for the first time. But she'd fallen asleep almost instantly, before she could celebrate or be aware of the fact. She had practically missed it, except now it was washing in her again as she remembered Angela's fingers inside her. Dark shapes flickered against the window. Flashes of brilliant white light lit the room.

"Do you know when this rain's going to stop?"

"I only know when it's starting."

They lay and looked at each other.

"Aren't you tired at all?"

"I think I'm hungry," Bonnie dared to say.

Angela sat up.

"I'll get you something."

She went downstairs, her lovely feet noiseless on the thick carpet. Once more Bonnie waited for someone to claim Angela from her. She still felt as though a mistake had been made. She wondered what Angela was doing down there, but then she was back, with cheese and olives and bread on a wooden board. And it was still just the two of them. *All this? for me?* Bonnie wanted to ask, as though it were a feast laid out on a long, candlelit table. They ate. Then Bonnie was thirsty. Angela went back down and made a gin and tonic which they passed between them. Angela spilt it on the sheet and they discussed the dangers of a gin and electric blanket short circuit. Bonnie felt herself couple to Angela. She felt herself latch and hold. Now there was no turning back. Her life spun on a fortune wheel and stopped at the notch that read 'complicated'.

Finally they slept, Bonnie's arm cushioned beneath Angela's head, the other arm curled around her belly.

The next morning Bonnie dreamed that she was a bird flying high above a coast somewhere. Through one eye she could see steep rugged cliffs and stunted trees. The other eye reflected the glitter of blue. She was weightless, gliding. Her arms flung themselves around the bed, pushing down phantom air currents.

While Bonnie was landing from her flying dream and opening her eyes to a strange room, Angela was smiling at the studio cameras. There was a full audience in the circus seats. The last clap faded and the audience sat stone still with faces that waited to be arranged. Today her own face was bursting with secrets. Her skin glowed.

*

Bonnie prowled through the house in a light that made the furniture solid and real, so now there were details she had missed last night. Angela's family smiled out at her from golden frames. There was Angela the little kid standing next to a younger girl and a boy with a dark scowl who must be Fourwords.

"Hello shithead," Bonnie said and then looked around, as if he might be standing in the doorway.

A man in corduroy jackets, variously green, brown or black was in the photos too. Maybe their father. Angela leaned against him trustingly. In one picture they stood on a wharf in front of a moored boat, the father's hand resting proudly on the boat's railing. Their eyes squinted against sun. Bonnie imagined the weekend sails up into Pittwater, barbecues on the shore.

A mother telling them to put insect repellent on.

In the lounge room, film posters hung in plain black frames. Bonnie had to crane her neck to see them. Rather than assume such a position of worship she took a step back to examine them. There was Angela holding a man by the hand. There she was again held in a tight embrace by another man. Her body and her smile had been pegged up for drying in a hundred dark rooms.

Bonnie sat on the white corduroy sofa and watched Angela's sparkling eyes on television.

"Hello! Welcome back," she said to Bonnie. Bonnie watched the performance through narrowed eyes. Trees outside tapped on the glass. This woman chose me for some reason, she thought. I go floating through life as though I'm on a river with things on the banks. Do I reach out for them or do they reach in for me?

A band came on and Bonnie leaned forward. The drummer was left-handed and had a strange way of arranging his cymbals. How fake it was, the way they were miming. The drummer touched his cymbals without hope or passion.

"Make an effort," Bonnie scolded aloud. "It's the least you can do."

Television's fakery didn't stop amazing her.

Angela came home with her body humming from work and found Bonnie asleep in front of the television wearing a blue silk shirt that she had pulled out of Angela's wardrobe. She grasped Angela sleepily, silk sleeves trailing, and felt Angela's excitement in the electricity of her clothing and her crackling hair. It woke her. Once again there were clothes to shed. Bonnie pushed the actress down onto the carpet and kissed her. Still the humming rose from Angela's body. So Bonnie began licking her until the saliva had washed off every smell and particle of fame. She bit gently but wanted to tear at her skin. Angela looked at her with bright eyes that never seemed startled or surprised.

Bonnie got on top of her and thought 'now you belong to me'.

She understood now the desire to own a body. The need to insist sexually as a reminder of previous intimacy. Fucking was a faster way of bonding than hours of soul-searching chat. As efficient as fighting, which she hadn't yet learned to do. Their skin and bones pushed and rubbed and locked. Their eyes and lips met and stayed. The sound of this friction and the sound of fast breathing added to desire. They took different routes and highways into sex, into each other. Bonnie discovered that coming with Angela meant she couldn't hide anything from her. It also meant she didn't want to. Good sex made her honest and brave. Angela ran a finger around Bonnie's right nipple.

"When I was doing the show today all I thought about was your face."

"What's wrong with the rest of me?"

"The rest of you is perfect."

"I found photos of your wedding."

"Ah."

"I wanted to rip them up."

"And did you?"

"No!" Bonnie was shocked. "Of course not."

"Did you have breakfast?"

They padded in to the kitchen. Angela cut into an orange and handed segments to Bonnie. Sprays of orange vapour exploded into the air. She made tea. They sat at the kitchen table and ate toast without speaking. Angela ran her hand down Bonnie's arm. It felt like water trickling from her shoulder to her wrist.

Angela's lust for Bonnie was continuous. They had sex for what seemed like days. Bonnie learned how her own sexual appetite awoke from just kissing, how it waited and then swelled and rose. She came fully and easily. They lay on the grass in the back yard and watched clouds puff and thin. The sun heated their skin until the smell of bed and sex rose from them like perfume.

The phone in the hall rang occasionally.

"Do you want to answer it?"

"No."

"Do you need to do anything? Be anywhere?"

"Not yet. Do you?"

"No."

They lay in bed and listened to the answering machine. Morgan called from New Zealand. His voice was cheerful.

"Hey, Angela! Don't forget to renew the household insurance. Use my card if you want. I forgot all about it. I'll be home on the seventeenth now, not the twelfth."

He called back.

"Hope you're having fun," was all he said. There was not even a twinge of irony.

"So are we insured?"

Angela smiled without opening her eyes. She lay on the bed, weighted down by Bonnie's head.

"No."

"We might get robbed."

Despite their exhaustion their sleep was thin and shallow. They woke each other up every time they turned over. Anything woke them — the street lights, sirens, the sounds of people walking past. Scraps of urgent conversation drifted up through the window.

" … tell her what you want if you're so angry …"

" … past the application date …"

And then they started talking in their own scraps.

"When Belle and I saw you at the studio Morgan was kissing someone in the green room."

Angela took the news with her usual calm.

"He's a careless boy sometimes."

Bonnie felt goose bumps rise on her arms.

"Why are you looking at me like that?"

Bonnie dropped her eyes but then looked up again.

"I feel like I need to know something about you. Personal stuff."

"You don't feel that you know me?"

"No."

"It's funny, I feel like I know you. I have the advantage I suppose."

"Why?"

"Let me tell you a story. Years ago I was in a theatre company that toured Queensland. There were five of us in this little theatre company. It was my first real acting job and it was fantastic. Three men and two women. We drove between a whole lot of tiny towns in outback Queensland. We played in halls to forty or fifty people every second night. The people that showed up were really hungry for — not drama — but some sort of show."

"Or maybe just new people to look at."

"The people who met us in each town always assumed we were in pairs, you know, two couples and one single man. But really there was one gay couple, one straight couple and one single person. At first I was homesick for Sydney. The heat was unbearable and we drank a lot. Then after we'd played in about seven towns I fell in love with Jude, the other actress."

Bonnie shifted. She was growing to hate stories told in bed.

"It took a while to realise it. She told me later she was waiting and waiting for me to make the first move. But it took me ages to cotton on. And then came the wondering period. You know the sort of thing? I wonder what Jude's doing, I wonder what Jude would think of this and that, etcetera. I looked forward to seeing her every day and I felt alive and happy when I was with her. All sure signs."

Angela tilted Bonnie's face up so she could stroke it.

"You look like her. You have her face. It's why I wanted to see you."

"Keep going."

"Onstage, Jude was fantastic. By far the best actor of all of us. Offstage she was witty and warm and funny. She and I always seemed to touch each other a lot. We started to kiss each other good night. Then we started to kiss each other good morning. We drove everyone mad because we acted like school kids. Eventually we held hands all the time. It was a path leading somewhere. We could feel it."

"But she was married."

"Yes. Anyway, we finally got drunk one night with everyone else. There was a big group of us as usual. The locals took us to wherever the action was which was always a pub with wooden floors and those big ceiling fans. Jude and I were holding hands and standing at the bar. We got drunk. Very drunk. Everyone else went to bed. The bar closed and the bar staff very politely threw us out. So we sat in the van and talked until 3 o'clock."

"Then what?"

"Then we got into the back of the van and had sex. Very uncomfortably. My brother found us there still asleep the next morning."

"What was he doing there?"

"He was her husband."

"Fourwords?"

"Yes. He pulled us out of the van and called us every name under the sun. We stood there and copped it. We were terrified of him and his rotten temper. The other boys dragged him off and calmed him down but the rest of the tour was appalling. Jude and I were a mess. She was so guilt ridden and I was confused about how I felt. The two boys counselled us all the time.'

"Did you keep having sex?"

"When we could, yes. I wanted to see if we could do it when we were sober. Everyone ignored Fourwords even though he was the aggrieved lover. He played it to the hilt. He kept sulking and getting drunk."

"How did he do the show if he was drunk?"

"It was a thriller called *The Face in The Window*. He didn't have a big part. He got murdered in the first five minutes and after that all you could see were his legs."

"Ha!"

"Sometimes he nodded off during the show and so we left him to sleep onstage all night. Jude and I slept together when that happened."

Angela mashed a pillow against her face and then took it away. She examined the pattern on it.

"Fourwords threatened to kill himself one afternoon by jumping off the edge of a viaduct. We'd stopped for lunch. He started saying 'why don't I just jump?' He had a sandwich in one hand. Jude walked over to calm him down. The rest of us sat in the van, bored by the whole thing. There was a beautiful view into a valley behind where they stood on the bridge and I remember thinking how silly humans were and their little dramas, getting all existential. I shouted 'Fine, take him back'. I was angry with her, sick of the whole business. Eventually he took her hand to climb back up and she fell backwards and over the edge."

"Jesus."

"She ended up in hospital. End of tour."

"She didn't die, did she?"

"No. She had a broken leg and broken ribs."

"Did you talk to her in hospital?"

"No. I haven't talked to her since."

"No wonder Fourwords hates me, if I look like her."

"He hates the world."

"Why did you marry Morgan?"

Angela looked at her, slightly puzzled, as if to say, 'isn't it obvious?' but didn't answer.

"What will you do now the show's finished?" she asked Bonnie.

"Find a band, I suppose."

'How do you make a living?"

"I clean offices."

"Why?"

"I want to be a drummer."

She realised how strange that sounded.

"Does that make sense to you?"

"As far as I can see you are a drummer, not someone wanting to be one."

What a great way to look at things, Bonnie thought.

She woke with her hands and feet tingling. Rhythms were invading her head like voices. She tapped her fingers on the sheet gently. It sounded like thunder or galloping horses. She experimented with the sheet held at different tensions. The pitch went higher, then lower. Angela turned and said without opening her eyes:

"You're getting restless. Go home. Ring me."

She was being dismissed.

Famous people chew you up and spit you out.

Bonnie drove Belle's ute back to her flat. The sun was pinging white against her eyeballs and she felt drained, hungry, tired. Older. Her pubic bone was sore to the touch and when she glanced at the rear view mirror, dark-circled eyes looked back at her.

"Lusty old dyke," she whispered. Darlinghurst still looked washed clean after the heavy rain of two nights ago. Her flat was dark, stuffy, neglected. She picked up her sticks and put a page of triplet patterns on the stand. 123123123123. The dots floated in front of her eyes. For the first time, Bonnie couldn't concentrate. She was full of Angela. Her skin, her voice, her taste. Angela had told her not to tell anyone.

"Can you promise me?"

Last line. 123 123 123 123. That was a fantastic rhythm if she could get it to sound the slightest bit even. Play it again. Push the woman out of your mind. "What about Belle? She knows."

"Tell her not to tell *anyone*."

123123123123123123123123.

"All right."

She disappeared behind the drum kit as she practised her triplets. Bodiless in public and an accessory to the main action on stage. When the phone rang Bonnie realised she had been sitting and staring again, like an animal frozen in headlights.

"Phone unanswered for two nights. Inference one —"

"Inference one, your best friend minding her own beeswax."

"I've been doing some asking around. Discreetly of course. If Angela sleeps with women on a regular basis she must fly to outer Siberia to do it."

"What do you mean?"

There was the hiss and crackle of Belle dragging on a badly rolled cigarette.

"I mean her record is flawless." She exhaled. "So what happened? Did anything happen?"

"Belle, you have to promise me that you will tell no-one."

"Wow!"

"No-one!"

Belle groaned. "I promise. Can I bring a bottle over? Or would I be disturbing something?"

Bonnie hung up. Belle would only get the truncated version of her and Angela's time together. What they had was a secret between them. It was not entertainment for Belle. She didn't have the right to a description of Angela's body or the tiny moles on her breasts and stomach. Or to the sensation of the soft valleys between her lips and her teeth. Bonnie smiled. They had coiled over around and under each other like hot, wet rope. Heat went through her just thinking about it. She felt a hundred years older, thick with old, wise blood.

But when Belle came to toast the occasion and pledge undying secrecy, Bonnie's mood had twisted. Here she was with another precious thing that was unsharable and unshowable. Somehow she would make it last. She felt the sweet wine pool and sour in her stomach.

*

Night cleaning spooked Bonnie but it paid well. It also gave her acres of beautiful silence. She emptied ashtrays into bins, emptied bins into larger bins in the waste rooms on every floor. She pushed a huge mop across the veined marble on the ground floor, teeth grinding away in rhythm. The rest

71

of the building was carpeted olive green and partitioned with grey baffle board.

Security guards walked through the maze of offices and sometimes in the absolute silence she could hear the dry click ... click of their heavy boots crossing the ground floor. Tonight she was so tired she didn't even jump when one of them suddenly appeared in front of her. He must have come out of the lift while she had the vacuum cleaner on.

"Hi," she said and the man nodded as he padded past. Now that he was level with her she could smell a sort of bachelor smell about him. His hair hung down between his shoulder blades and was tied in a careless pony tail. There was the burst and crackle of a short wave radio. He pushed it against his mouth.

"Just the cleaner up here," he told it. Just the cleaner indeed.

At twelve o'clock she took a break on one of the long benches that lined the wall of the first floor. From her rucksack she pulled out an apple and *How to Play Drums*. For a book with such a babyish name it has some hard stuff in it. It was not one of the books that Charlie had recommended to her and, following some sort of instinct, she hadn't told him about it. She had the vague idea that the rolls in it were out of date, the way that herbs and medicine could become out of date: outwardly fresh but stale and possibly dangerous if used. She yawned as she flicked through it. She could barely keep her eyes open to read the patterns.

She dozed off.

"Hey!"

She snapped awake. The security guard was standing in front of her. He had changed into jeans but he still wore a Security Company's khaki shirt with the red and white logo. His shift must have finished.

She looked at the logo: "We care." But this bloke didn't look as if he did.

"This yours?"

He handed her *How To Play Drums* and she bent to put it in her rucksack. There was an awkward silence. When she looked up he was still there.

"God!" she said into this chasm of quiet. "I must have nodded off!"

How long had he been watching her?

"Do you?"

"Do I what?"

"Play drums."

"Yeah, I do."

"You really play that marching band sort of shit? Fancy rolls and stuff like that? Are you in a military band?"

"No. I play ..."

What did she play? She felt herself waking up slowly.

"I've played in musicals. Just finished one last week. Looking for other work at the moment."

She heard herself take on his lazy speech.

"Did you know you always nod your head when you're cleaning?"

"No."

"Like you got a band happening inside there somewhere. Play rock n roll?"

"Well I like it, I spose."

"Funk?"

"Yes. I like Stanley Clarke."

To her surprise he smiled.

"Check this out then."

He led her to the end of the corridor and through a small door that opened into a small kitchen. At the end of the kitchen was another door. Locked. He stood and fiddled with a bunch of keys. The lock was intricate and heavy duty.

"Who've you got in there? James Brown?"

He opened the door. It was a large broom cupboard. A bass guitar leaned against one wall. A small amp squatted on the floor. There were other bits and pieces that she recognised. A tuner, a set of strings. A stool. No order, no design.

"I practise in here sometimes."

"Don't people hear you?"

"Pitt Street at three in the morning?"

He squeezed into the small space, sat down and picked up the guitar. He reached over and turned up the volume on the amp just a fraction. Then he played, not a tune but various scales with a pattering and popping of strings. There were accents in strange places. A perfect execution of scales customised to suit his taste and relieve the tedium of practice.

"That's great."

He didn't hear her. He kept playing, his gaze was fixed somewhere at her knees, and his eyes were wide and trancelike.

"Listen. I've got to go," she said.

He stopped playing and hooked his right thumb onto the top string.

"I play with a guy called The Martyr who's a guitarist. He thinks he's Hendrix but try and find one who doesn't. Anyway he's got us some work at The Exeter in George Street."

The Martyr?

"That's good."

He shook his head.

"It'll be foul. We're not a duet. It's not how the songs are written. We need a drummer. One we had moved to Queensland. Got some crappy Gold Coast gig."

73

He looked up at her. He seemed to be in pain.

"Do you want to do it?"

Oun car!!!

"I don't have a car."

"I've got a Combi. Could keep your kit in there for a while. You have a kit, don't you?"

"Have you got a tape that I could listen to?"

He scrabbled around in the back of the amp.

"Thought I had one … ah!"

He handed her a cassette. A tiny silver moon with golden red flames decorated the cover. A halo of musical and astrological symbols surrounded the word 'Firetown'. It was beautiful. She stared at it.

"Nice cover."

"Makes it look like an ambient tape."

"It's beautiful."

"The Martyr churns them out."

He was determined to down play.

"He hand painted all of them?"

"All fifty of em. He's got time on his hands. The ones we sent to the record companies were better than that even."

He sounded proud now.

"Have a listen. Quality's all right. It was done on a 16 track."

"All right."

She finished vacuuming with the tape shoved awkwardly in her overalls pocket and then caught the lift down to the marbled ground floor, her eyes dry with exhaustion. The small of her back ached. Another security guard let her out into the cold two a.m. air of Pitt Street.

She knew the band was called Firetown but she didn't know the bass player's name. She started walking toward Martin Place. Had he in fact told her his name? She could remember The Martyr, whatever that was. Moonlight had found its way into the canyons between the skyscrapers. The road in front of her was lit up. Maybe his name was Peter. She imagined the interviews.

"Pete and I hooked up in Sydney back in 1983. There was no-one playing what we played. It was all New Order, China Crisis, Yazoo. Keyboards everywhere."

"How do you find touring?"

"Exhausting, especially since we've been playing stadiums. We're thinking of going back to small rooms for a while."

"And that sound! That amazing Firetown feel. How long did it take to –"

A car pulled into the kerb in front of her. Now that was the sort of car she would own. A small white BMW, not too showy. The rear tyre shrieked and scraped against concrete guttering. The front tyre was out at least two feet but the driver didn't try to repark. He jumped out and left his beautiful car skew-whiff. He wore a pinstriped suit. He looked like the manager of some large bank, except the banks were shut for another seven hours. A phantom banker, a ghost in Pitt Street, was walking towards her. She should be worried. He got closer to her and smiled.

She. It was Angela.

I'm seeing things, thought Bonnie. Until Angela had her arms around her and Bonnie smelt her body. She sniffed her in. Welcomed her in.

"I've tracked you down." Angela's purring voice was muffled.

"You could, the way I smell."

Sweat, floor polish, dust.

"So why didn't you ring me?"

Bonnie tried to shrug but she was still drowning in pin stripes. So she told herself: I thought you were just saying it. I didn't know your number. And underneath that: I thought you called all the shots because you're famous. Angela released her and looked at her and kissed her and squeezed her hand. Looking, squeezing, kissing. Everything was happening at once, including the slow wash of arousal.

"I had to ring Belle to find you."

"What did she say?"

"She said you were bloody hopeless. And shy."

Belle would have wavered between curious questions and pompous advice.

"And she told me your cleaning hours at the bank."

Bonnie felt humiliated. No-one else had made her feel that, not even her mother who had been shocked that her daughter would choose to clean banks.

"She asked me if I could get you work in a musical."

Bonnie felt embarrassment burn even deeper. It was as though she were standing in a mud-filled pit while people with shovels tried to dig her out. They walked towards the car.

"She shouldn't have done that."

"Why not?"

"I hate favours like that. I'd never ask you for that."

"Look, it's OK. Really. It's how the world works."

"So are we still seeing each other?'

Angela leaned Bonnie against the car and stroked her face, pulled her hair back so that her skin was taut. She kissed her. Whisky, thought Bonnie. Some sort of strange energy was emanating from Angela. Her public body was thrumming with animation.

"I've just been to an awards night. I had to present an award for most promising young talent of 1983."

She squeezed Bonnie's hand while she spoke, as though the hand was rock that might eventually drip a seam of rich gold.

"I stood there and I thought 'fuck, I need to see Bonnie'. So yes, we are still seeing each other. Is it still what you want?"

The word *fuck* flowered into an exotic vine in Angela's mouth. Bonnie hung between several quick responses. She waited for herself to speak, as though she were two people.

"Yeah of course."

"Let's go then."

They spent another clump of numberless days together. They drove up to the mountains and watched snow fall through trees and ate in restaurants in front of people whose eyes slid past Bonnie, stared at Angela and then slid back to Bonnie. They walked through the bush while birds as small as leaves darted between branches, tails flipped up like warning fingers.

"Can you predict snow as well as rain?"

"No."

Bonnie held out cupped hands but the flakes melted to crystals that disappeared into her skin before they could gather.

They were staying in Blackheath in a hotel whose walls were papered gold-red and icy to the touch. The corridors wound like ribbons to the left and right and at the end of one day's walk, when they were tired and hungry, Bonnie and Angela lost their way to their room. Every door had the same crazed wood panelling. Once inside, with the door shut, they wrapped themselves around each other. They lay on the bed and watched the winter light thicken and grow dark. Angela's fingers were never far from Bonnie's face. Outside, fog or chimney smoke drifted past, low to the ground.

"Why can't I get enough of you? You make me feel like a lecherous old woman."

"You are a lecherous old woman."

Angela bit and tickled her.

"Ah!" Bonnie shouted. "Get off me."

It was good to yell. She felt an elation, an astounding happiness that Angela wanted her and that they were here. It was the rarest thing, this contentment with here and now. She bent over Angela's handsome face. She wanted to say 'I love you'. She opened her mouth but Angela put a hand over it.

"Let's go and eat."

"Haven't we just eaten?"

"That was hours ago. Let's eat dinner downstairs."

The dining room was full of people with faces flushed either from the heat in the room or from fast illicit sex. There was a smell of warm damp wool and thick onion soup. They sat at a table next to the window. Outside, pine needles swayed and tipped with crusts of ice. Bonnie spidered her right hand across the table and stroked Angela's knuckles. Angela moved her hand to pick up the menu.

"Their porterhouse steak is excellent."

"Is it?"

Bonnie ordered steak and then lay her warm right hand flat against the window glass. It was like a sheet of smooth ice, so cold that her palm hurt.

They drove back to the city the next day. As it grew warmer Bonnie stowed her jumper in her rucksack and felt something hard and smooth between her fingers. It was the cassette. Firetown. She looked at the names of the songs. 'How the World Works', 'Dots Are Joined'.

"Can I put this on?"

"Sure."

At first there was the sound of talking. It cut off abruptly and then a guitar played a long chord, rich with resonance. It held for ages and then the familiar busy bass she'd heard in the bank storeroom came up underneath it, popping away, teasing the guitar with its speed. A moment later the guitar took off with the bass and they continued in perfect time. They chased each other, swooping like two swallows. Bonnie played with them, ignoring the drum machine that was ticking away. She played it all out in her head. She knew exactly what she would do if she were there with them and behind a drum kit. She would be a rock. A constant presence but not invisible. Not with this music. She would be the centre, the eye of the storm.

"Do you like it?"

"There's no singing."

Bonnie laughed and Angela looked over at her.

"Who is it anyway?"

"It's my new band."

77

5

The bass player's name was Saul. The guitarist who hand painted the moons and symbols, The Martyr, was a left-handed player and was thin and tall with long pony-tailed hair like Saul's. He hated being left-handed, he told her, but he seemed to hate a lot of things and spent most of his non-playing time listening to a walkman. At first Bonnie was wary of him but then as she listened to his rare sentences, as carefully manicured as his lyrics, she realised his silences were due to his lisp. And acute introversion. The Martyr avoided ess words or, most of the time, all words. He didn't realise that it made people look into his face and listen to him even more carefully.

Saul was awkward too. At their first meeting in Saul's flat the three of them slid their eyes down and sideways and studied the walls as they talked. By the end of the hour Bonnie knew each bit of dust, cable end and wrinkled gaffer tape on the floor. Later she could describe to Belle how many power points ran along the dirty skirting boards, the colour of the blue-green carpet and grey-white walls but not the faces of the two men she had decided to play with.

"What a bunch of sad cases." Belle was disgusted.

"Not really. If the lights had blown we would've found our way out easily."

But it changed. It changed as soon as they played together in the rehearsal studio where the caretaker sat and watched his portable TV while bands loaded in and out. After they had played one song, the one Bonnie had first heard as she sat in the car, Saul and The Martyr looked at each other.

"All right!" Saul said.

The Martyr nodded.

"Four drummers we've had. Four fucking drummers."

She looked at them both while she blew on her hands. She wondered where the other drummers were now and what the arguments had been. These two, with their hair the same length and the same black shirts, were like an old married couple fussy about company.

"What? What is it?"

"Where'd you learn to play?"

"He likes your drumming," Saul said. "So do I. You don't play every other bloody drum every four seconds."

"Do you like ours?"

Like a lot of laconic people The Martyr was blunt to the point of dullness.

"Yes, I do."

"Join the band then," Saul said. There was silence as everyone looked at everyone else. Saul pulled at a clot of his hair.

"But Firetown's a pathetic name," said The Martyr. "Don't you reckon? Pass us the tuner Saul."

"OK, I'm in."

They played for another hour and in three songs Saul sang with a voice that was high and sad. She couldn't understand a lot of the words but his bass guitar still galloped along like a horse under a panicked rider. In between songs Saul and The Martyr argued listlessly, not out of anger but to anchor themselves when they came out of playing.

"Why do you always stuff up that E before the bridge?"

"Can't be perfect the whole time."

"I know *that.*"

"All right then, why do you always speed up during your solos?'

"But you *always* stuff up that one note –"

And then into the next song and they would lose everything else.

Now that she was part of them she felt forgotten. But she was like an arm that opened doors, started cars, stirred pots. If she stopped stirring the pots, the music would gum up.

What if they put the hard word on her, she thought later as she lay in bed listening to the fridge go whirr clunk whirr. Her back and wrists ached in the cold of her flat.

But they didn't put the hard word on her. Her role as the drummer made her sexless somehow, or a sister. And they never mentioned lovers they might have. At the bank she and Saul sat close together on the benches in the dead of night and talked in low voices about Firetown. When he talked to her now he spoke in full sentences. He had a philosophy about success.

"If you crave success you can go mad when you get it. I know. I've played in famous bands with guys that don't know who they are any more. They think that they'll solve everything with fame and when they don't and they have the same crummy lives and attitudes —" he flicked the fingers of one hand out and up. "Everything goes up in smoke. Years of sweat and blood."

"The money would help though," she hoped.

"I'm thirty years old now." He looked grim. "I'm giving myself another five years to make it."

He looked down at his black desert boots.

"Actually no. I give myself this band. If Firetown doesn't work out I'm doing something else."

"Course you'll make it. You're a great bass player."

"That's not enough. I was in a great band. We were all bloody virtuosos but it wasn't enough."

"What would you do instead?"

"I'd do a real estate course. Or maybe architecture. Buildings are pretty good, I reckon."

He would wander aimlessly, she could tell. And then he would come back to playing music.

"If you weren't playing you'd go spare," she told him.

"How do you know?"

"Cause I feel the same way."

In the bank at night, rhythms drove through her like tracks.

"You're bloody good, you know. We've had drummers who talked about how they had maple wood shells and Japanese White Oak sticks. Brand names were all they worried about. And what they looked like. I remember one drummer who was really bad. Mate he thought he was the best! He had a necklace with little gold drumsticks hanging off it."

That sounded nice, she thought. Little gold drumsticks.

"You came along and picked things up just like that. You know what to hit when. And when to shut up and keep it basic."

"But that's not enough."

He laughed in his throat.

One night they went postering through the streets. At the first telegraph she nearly dropped everything when a car slowed to watch them. Then they ran to the next pole. Then the next. They got into a rhythm. She unpeeled a poster from the stack between her legs and hugged it to the wood, then arched out again while Saul looped sticky tape round and round the pole, making a sound like screaming, tearing paper. They covered only one suburb before chucking it in and buying coffee at a petrol station, shivering and aching at a table edged in aluminium. Exhaustion made the light hurt their eyes.

"Wouldn't be dead for quids," said Saul with his hands clamped under his armpits.

"Me neither."

She was nodding off into her cup. The rising steam jarred her awake and upright.

"Hey Bonnie, promise me something."

"What?"

"Promise me you're not the sort of person who's scared of being famous."

"I doubt that!"

"I want to make sure you won't run away or break down or pick fights if the band makes it."

"I wouldn't do that."

Why would she pick a fight? People who went with the flow didn't have fights.

"I put my music before my relationships. It's my number one priority."

He didn't seem to believe that anyone else could want what he wanted as much as he did. To tell the truth, she wasn't sure she did. He had the fervour of a religious zealot except that he always unravelled his ideas and his dreams quietly and in corners, not on a stage or a pulpit. She gave up trying to reassure him.

Their first gig was in a week.

*

Bonnie knew finally that drumming had been the right decision. She felt the smug sweet-tasting difference between sensing it when no-one else had and watching everyone gradually realise it. Firetown were doing well. The Martyr still grumbled and whinged with Saul at rehearsal but now they argued about management as well as craft. Their second demo tape landed them regular work. With her share of the money Bonnie bought new drum heads, a variety of oak and hickory drum sticks and an aluminium cylinder that clamped to wherever she wanted so she could store sticks there for the times when she broke or dropped one in mid song.

"What about stage gear?" Belle wanted to know, following Bonnie around a drum shop one day.

"This is stage gear."

Belle exhaled frustrated air.

"Clothes, I mean. Stage clothes." She picked at the corner of a row of black T shirts.

"I've got clothes. You think I'd play naked?"

"Do they know you're a lesbian yet?" Belle asked while Bonnie was looking at sticks.

"No, why?"

"Are you going to tell them?"

"No."

"Why not?"

"Why should I? It's no big deal."

"Then tell them. Just say: hey, did you guess I'm a lesbian yet?"

"Why?"

"It's important?"

"Why?"

"Because all around the word there are women saying it's no big deal, when actually it is a big deal. It's a huge deal."

"Belle, don't give me grief over this."

Belle threw her hands up in the air in a backing off motion.

Bonnie bought a spare snare drum and a spare kick pedal, not luxuries but necessities. And cases for her toms. Firetown were playing three or four times a week and her equipment was dragged, dropped and thrown around in the back of Saul's Combi and down rehearsal room stairs. Rehearsals gradually became more streamlined, songs tightened and new ones seemed to write themselves. Their song list grew from eight to fifteen. From fifteen to twenty. At rehearsals there was a sense of wonderful focus. It was serious. No games were played. They actually created things.

"You know that riff you played the other day?" Saul would say to The Martyr.

"Which one?" his fingers ready on the frets.

"Barm bup bup bup bup barm bup bup."

Saul sang it without any sense of comedy. Bonnie would have laughed except they were both so intent on the noise coming from him, The Martyr leaning forward watching Saul's mouth, nodding. As if he knew exactly which riff Saul meant among twenty that he fiddled with. He thought for a minute and played a hoppy little melody.

"Yeah! Yeah! Keep going."

And Saul joined in and then Bonnie stopped thinking and started up a tentative beat on the kick and hi-hat or the kick and snare, and Saul would smile and nod and there was half a song already.

People offered to manage them. Women stepped up to Bonnie while she was packing up and talked to her about the drum kits they'd just bought, or wanted to buy. Did she teach? they asked. They gave her telephone numbers but she never rang them. Except once she wanted to, because she had liked the woman. She'd bought a bass drum and snare drum at a garage sale. What else did she need before she could play? she asked Bonnie. She was too shy to walk into a drum shop, she said. Such uncertainty appealed to Bonnie. She'd scrabbled through her jeans but the paper scrap with her number on it must have fluttered out.

The Martyr wore his walkman less often.

"We're being feted," he said. "Never thought the day would come."

They were interviewed by music magazines.

"How do you get your song ideas?" one woman asked.

"Bonnie has six million rhythms in her head," Saul said when no-one else answered. "She pulls one out and away we go."

Bonnie gathered her eyebrows at him. The journalist looked at her notepad. She had questions like a shopping list down the page.

"Tell me about your lyrics."

"I read a lot so that's where they come from," Saul said. "But they're not so important. Song titles are crucial though."

"Who do you read?"

"American writers. Poets too. I love American writers."

Saul enjoyed interviews but the other two hung back, The Martyr mindful of his esses and wary of the journalist, Bonnie chewing on the collar of her jacket, her mind blank.

"Just make up anything," Saul said to them. "You have to get used to interviews."

"Listen to Mr Experience," said The Martyr.

"At least pretend to be interesting."

One journalist keen to make a mark gave the band a fancy tag.

Hung in the balance between predictable Australian pub rock and pop synth Firetown have managed to invent, and survive on, their own brand of psychedelic funk music. They are playing the baby that James Brown and Jimi Hendrix never had. Lean, fluid and danceable, psychafunk may be here to stay.

Bonnie and Saul laughed and laughed at that. The Martyr frowned and read the article once more.

"Psychafunk. That's all right. That's good," he said.

Bonnie wondered about Belle's question. Did these boys need to know she was a lesbian? Why had Belle asked, do they know yet?

Angela and Bonnie saw each other every three or four days in between *Sunday Live* and Firetown. Bonnie felt that somehow their relationship was more equal. She felt more worthy of Angela. She felt spilling over with love, keen to share herself now there was something else to share, now that she was enriching herself by playing and performance. She wanted to show herself off.

"Come to a gig. Come on!"

"The cigarette smoke gives me headaches."

"No-one'll recognise you."

"No."

Bonnie gave up.

One night Bonnie asked Saul to drop her off in front of Angela's house. They had headlined for the first time that night and a lot of people showed up. Saul and The Martyr wanted to go to the Manzil Room to celebrate.

"Don't you want to come?"

"I'll be there a bit later."

The Combi burbled off and she stood on the footpath in an outsider's stance, one leg rubbing shyly against the other. Two upper windows glowed yellow. Angela's bedroom light and the one at the other end of the second floor – the light of Morgan's study. He had his own part of the house, like the mad wife in Jane Eyre.

Bonnie felt like a moth at the flame. Her ears rang in the silent street. She would wait until Morgan went to his room before she climbed over the wall. She watched his window, willing him to feel tired, to go to sleep. Ah! A shadow loomed against the glass, silhouetted by a backlight. It changed shape as it rose higher and closer to the glass and Bonnie recognised the pointed bristly beard of Morgan. The light in his study went out. A hall light went on. Bonnie waited for the light in his bedroom to come on but his shadow flickered and travelled towards Angela's room. The hall light went off and in the rubbery time that shock induces, Bonnie didn't know if two minutes or two hours had passed when Angela's bedroom went black. The house stood like a tomb.

She stumped home along Edgecliff Road and down the expressway opposite Rushcutters Bay. Men shouted from cars. Her gymboots, that she wore so that she could feel the drum pedals beneath her feet, had always made walking a joy. Now she could feel every stone on the road. The security doors were almost too heavy to open. The key slipped and scratched in the lock. Her ears were still ringing when she fell into bed and imagined Morgan fucking her girlfriend.

*

Nora and Melanie came to see Firetown. They sometimes brought clowning and potting friends and sat down at a table, squinting through the smoke. Bonnie could see them straight away from where she sat behind her kit at the back of the stage. Their clothes flared bright red and yellow like beacons in a sea of black.

In the break they reported their observations to Bonnie, like the outsiders they were. They shook their heads and marvelled at some of the haircuts.

"A few more dykes here than last time."

"Can't you tell the audience not to smoke while you play? I don't know how you breathe up there."

"Course she can't!" Melanie said. "They're paying customers."

Melanie went to the bar to buy more beer.

Nora reached over and took Bonnie's hand.

"It's a shame you don't have anyone to share all this with, Bon. All this glory."

"It's all right."

"Someone you could go home and unwind with."

Was Nora fishing around for information? Bonnie held the secret of Angela close.

"I've got the boys," she said brightly.

Nora raised her eyebrows. "Of course. Silly me. I suppose they know about you?"

"What about me?"

"I'm back." Melanie skidded fresh bottles onto their table. "Hey, Bonnie, I heard a woman back there say that she knew you from school."

"Yeah? Where?"

Melanie nodded towards a woman at the end of the bar. She was leaning across to pick up a wineglass. Bonnie recognised her in a second. The way she picked the glass up with one hand and daintily straightened her skirt with the other was unmistakable. Even across the room.

"No, I don't know her."

"Maybe she was pretending to know you to impress someone."

"Yeah, maybe."

Bonnie felt too shy to walk over and talk to Jane Gannon. Not shy. Scared. She looked at Nora to see if she had seen her too but Nora was sitting and staring at the label on her imported beer.

"That's outrageous. An extra two dollars for a beer with a picture of a bear on it. Shows what some fancy wrapping can do."

Jane must be here to see someone else, not her.

*

It was all too easy. It felt like beginner's luck that kept stretching to accommodate more and more good fortune. She moved into a larger flat and bought a real bed and a fridge, still old, that didn't go whirr clunk whirr. She missed the rhythms of her old bedsit until she heard carpentry in the flat below her. Hammer on wood. Someone else, an old woman, had a walking stick that she used to tap her way up and down the hall stairs. The rhythm was maddeningly incomplete to Bonnie – an irregular tap, click, slide that repeated until the woman reached her own flat. Ghostly relentless rhythms were all around her, she realised. No need to worry about running out of them. She sang little songs to herself when she drove Saul's Combi. When he wasn't there of course.

Got me a woman
Got me a fine woman
Got me a band
Got me a fine band
We're playin' up a ladder
(grinding gears)
Moving that ladder
Groovin that thing

Senseless, stupid songs that made her happy. Must get her own car, she thought, and then she'd sing as loud as she liked. In the back her drums rocked as she cornered sharply.

Firetown got a manager. It was getting serious all of a sudden, the larger crowds, the larger rooms, the bigger PAs. And now a manager whose name was Phil.

"You'll be leaving your day jobs in three months, I guarantee it," he said.

Phil had perfected the art of the three day growth and was on trial with Firetown for six months. He had managed bands in England, he said. Ska bands. He had the look but really he was an unknown quantity. His receding mouse-brown hair and winning smile were the only solid things about him. His baggy trousers and waistcoats were vapour from another era.

"Bonnie and I have night jobs, not day jobs," Saul said.

The Martyr looked panicked.

"I don't have any bloody job."

Phil jingled change in his pockets like a father pondering the best way to spend money on his kids.

"You do now."

The three of them poked fun at Phil but he seemed to expect it and took on the earnest role that they wanted him to have. In return they accepted half of his proposals. He organised a roadie for Bonnie because, he said, it was a bad look for her to be lugging her own kit. She pretended reluctance and showed him muscles built up from lugging. He shook his head vigorously.

"Those muscles are from the playing itself. If I held my arms in mid air for two hours a day I'd have those muscles too. You'll only lose those if you give up drumming."

He rang people during sound checks and tried to bring industry heavies in to watch them play. He talked about image. Videos. He bustled through the Sydney heat in his English trousers, carrying a briefcase. He organised a photo session, the three of them sprawled and bland against a factory wall, and sent press releases to newspapers.

One day he toiled up the wooden stairs of the studio to their ugly rehearsal room and sat and listened for a while. It was something he never did. They felt self-conscious with him there and kept making false starts into songs. Bonnie realised what a private thing it was, not the performing of music but the making of it. It was something she did not want witnessed. There was a pathetic element about something that might not ever get heard.

She imagined all the musicians who'd ever sung or played in this room suddenly all there together, edgy with longing, practising for something, pushing each other out of the way. How many of them would be female? The small room was stuffy with dead air and hope.

Phil fidgeted politely against the wall until they asked him what was up. He stood and jammed his hands in his pockets.

"We need famous people to come and see you. Start a vibe happening. Do you know anyone famous?"

Saul and the Martyr considered the ridiculous question for a minute and shook their heads.

"I do," she said it before thinking.

"Do you? Who?"

"An actress."

"Can you arrange for her to come along and see the band?"

He left them to it and went off to organise a PA system. They listened to his pockets jingle along the hall and down the stairs. Saul leaned his bass against the amp and dug a packet of peanuts from his pocket.

"So, who's the actress?"

"You'll know her when you see her."

"But will she come? Does she like music?"

He munched his way to the bottom of the packet and upended it over his mouth. Downstairs a heavy metal band repeated the same riff over and over. Dar blang tickaticka blang. Dar blang tickaticka blang. Bonnie thought of Angela lying on her long white lounge listening to Sibelius. 'The Swan of Tuonela'.

"Yeah, she likes music."

But she had said it too carefully. Saul knew her well enough to feel the artifice.

"What's her name?"

The Martyr said: "Can we get on with it? I don't give a shit who she is. I just want to drown out those fuckers downstairs."

"I'm just curious," mumbled Saul and picked up his bass again. "I love movies."

*

On Saturday morning she bought a leather jacket from a Kings Cross pawn shop. Then she went to a barber shop and had her hair cut. She looked at herself in the mirror, still with the hairdresser's cape on, and went red with embarrassment. Her hair was transparent. It was as short and prickly as velvet and it sent up a flare that signalled 'lesbian here'. Her scalp was visible in strange pink patches.

She walked into the sound check, tried to look nonchalant, scuffed her feet on the stained carpet. Saul and The Martyr stared at her.

"Just as well you're thin," the Martyr said, "otherwise you'd look like a pinhead."

"You're just in time. The engineer wants you up there."

Bonnie sat behind the kit and beat slow time with her right foot. The engineer was not someone they'd used before. Saul knew him from somewhere and he had tonight as a try out. He looked ratty, tired and not recovered from whatever his Friday night had been.

"Snare drum."

Her left stick came down and made the snare crack like a whip around the room. The support band were watching her. They had done their sound check already and were hanging around for God knows what reason. Bonnie wished they'd go.

"First tom."

The Martyr and Saul lounged around a table smoking. The Martyr's headphones were planted in both ears as usual. Saul was doing a *Herald* crossword but sat in a listening posture.

"Play some time."

A cigarette dangled from her lip. She set up a brisk beat.

"That kick drum sounds terrible," he called out.

"It shouldn't. It's been tuned."

At the other end of the hall she saw his mouth twist in an unbelieving line.

"Just play your kick."

She pressed her foot down on the pedal again and again, grumbling quietly to herself. Other musicians could purr their arguments into a vocal mike if the engineer picked on their sound but drummers had to shout their defence from behind their kit right down to the back of the room.

The bass drum had a voice but he was right, it sounded off. More like a flat bump than its usual boom.

"Maybe it's the wrong mike in there," she said.

"Maybe you can't tune your kit." It was just a mumble from behind the desk.

Out of the corner of an eye she saw Saul sit up straight. Bonnie got up from the stool, walked to the front of her kit and peered into the bass drum. She unclipped the long thin mike from the stand and held it up above her head.

"Hey! Excuse me but isn't this a snare drum mike?"

The engineer scowled. Saul rose from his chair and turned to look at him.

"You dickhead! Go and fix the bloody mikes."

"Shit! Sorry man." The engineer grinned at Saul as he walked past. She walked to the side of the stage to give him space but knew by the way he moved close to her what he was about to spit out. Was waiting for it.

A lower-than-a-whisper aside for her ears only.

"Fucking dyke."

Delivered from the corner of his mouth. Her body glowed with shame and horror. Her hand moved up to touch her scalp. He jumped back off the stage and slouched clownishly back to the mixing desk. The man had known how to unload his venom – it coiled as heavy as guilt in her stomach. Saul gave him a playful punch in the arm as he passed him.

"What were you up to last night Glenn? Take too much marching powder?"

There was a snigger all round.

The Martyr and Saul checked their guitars and the band played two or three songs. Her tempo was sluggish. They looked at her curiously.

"You're lagging," Saul murmured from the corner of his mouth. But she knew, she knew, and was helpless.

Then the song raced. She felt the tempo drop away from her like a baton from a relay runner. Saul was working hard now to nail it down. She'd lost her confidence. As the song finished, silence dropped down onstage. The Martyr coughed without sounding like he really needed to.

"Let's try another one."

"OK," she said.

"'The Attack'?"

"Sure." It was an old song that she knew as well as her own hands. She counted it in all right and then tried to shake the fog that had settled like a chill into her legs and arms. Let go of it, let go, she told herself. Anger helped if she used it like petrol to fuel herself. She played better but something hard clenched inside her for the rest of the day.

That night she remained sober and clear. Things registered themselves coldly and cleanly as she played. Faces like pale flowers looking up at the stage. Phil standing and watching with an anxious face as usual. Saul's bass very loud. She moved up the cliff face without panic, the tempo still in her hands.

The sound man was a dark shape above the desk. That's all he was. In the break she bought Saul a bourbon.

"Thanks. You showed Glenn up today. He's looking as sour as an old goat."

For Saul it was a game of soldiers. Attack, retreat. Laugh it off.

"He's a sexist shit."

"He's a bullshit artist from way back. Don't take any notice."

Bonnie cracked ice between her teeth. She wondered how far she could take this.

He's a sexist shit.

Take no notice.

I don't want to use him for any more gigs.

But he's good.

It's him or me, Saul.

Aren't you overreacting a bit? He just used the wrong mike.

He called me a fuckin dyke.

I always wondered. Are you?

"It's hard. I get psyched out pretty easily, I think."

"Did he say something to you?"

They looked at each other, still standing at the bar. Hands pushed at the small of her back. Orders were shouted past her for two beers, three beers, two cokes. She washed tea-coloured bourbon down her throat in a large gulp.

"We should go back on."

But Saul was waiting for her answer. One thing about you, she thought. You listen. The Martyr wriggles and fidgets but you listen like a guard dog to a new noise. Tell him now, she told herself. Tell him.

"No, he didn't say anything. C'mon let's go."

The Martyr was pacing the stage impatiently but enjoying eye contact with women in the front. He was safe up there where people couldn't talk to him. Where his lisp couldn't be noticed. Bonnie scuttled behind her kit and with her gym boot pushed her song list to where she could read it. She picked up her sticks.

"Welcome back," Saul muttered into the mike. He was the same onstage as off, with his smiling grimness, his little ironies. Faces looked up at him. He scratched his head and then sighed as he strapped his bass on.

"Got your drinks? S'pose we have to play again ... now let's see."

He pretended to think what. The Martyr rolled his eyes at Bonnie and she grinned back over her cymbals. It was like waiting for the starting gun.

"'How the World Works'." someone yelled.

But it was 'Repeat and Forget' that was next on the song list. She was about to count it in when someone called out "'Mantelpiece' please."

"Yeah. Let's do Mantelpiece." said Saul to the two of them. Good! They pounced on it. Bonnie climbed. This was a song she had built and she knew its frame in her bones as if it was what held her up. Almost her favourite – enough to look forward to reaching it on the song list. Saul had written strange lyrics for this, about books and an axe that lived together above a fire place.

Her eyes swung from side to side. Wanting to connect with someone. The tall shape behind the mixing desk was obscured by dancers. She had forgotten him anyway. Their roadie stood against the wall, a drum key shining around his neck.

Her mind roamed. She was meeting Belle tonight at a bar called Celia's. She hadn't seen Belle for ages; she was working on a film as a third assistant director or something. The Martyr turned to look at Bonnie. Sweat had roped his hair. His name was really Martin, she'd found out. Guitarists and their wanky stage names. Why didn't he call himself Martin?

"Martin's an accountant's name," he'd told her. He shaped himself around his ambition. Even his Cuban-heeled boots were props. Except the lisp, she thought. That was his former self hanging around to remind him.

Funny the way this band was so close when they played. Like three legs on the same animal, driving differently but still moving the body forward. The Martyr and Saul often turned to watch her thrash away behind the kit as if for reassurance. It was as though they played to each other and kept the audience out. But after gigs they went separate ways like a family dissolving after breakfast.

When they came off stage forty minutes later Bonnie's hands shook from the blood running through them. Phil herded them into the tiny dressing room.

"There's a man from Rubber Records here who wants to talk to you."

He jingled his pockets ceremoniously. The man from Rubber Records stood and smiled at them. He smiled at Bonnie and looked at her hair.

"Hi. I'm Tony."

He looked like a musician who had done well. He wore the long-sleeved, silk shirt of a keyboard player who didn't have to throw his arms around or carry anything. His hair was receding at the front and was long at the back. He was growing a pony tail (was there any man who wasn't?) and looked like he would promise them things. Three shot glasses of Sambuca were on the table next to him.

"Saul is it? Here you go. Martyr? And … ?"

"It's Bonnie," Phil said.

"That's right." Tony handed her the glass. "Cheers everyone."

"Maybe I should change my shirt first," Bonnie said. Her shirt was limp with sweat but she drained the glass anyway.

"No, no. Please. As you are," Tony said and Saul's eyes said to her, don't you go anywhere.

"I'll keep it short. I'm sure you have things to do."

"Not really," said The Martyr, "we've got a roadie."

"I came here tonight because there's a bit of a vibe happening about you guys."

Phil turned his lips up in a smile.

"And I wanted to check you out for myself. You're good. Good feel, good playing. You look a bit scruffy but scruffy seems to be the go at the moment. Careful dressing is out. Torn T shirts are back and whatever else but anyway," he stopped to breathe, "I want to make a demo. Take you into a studio, leave you there for a while and see what comes out. Not just any old demo but an excellent demo. With a producer. Maybe Guy Anthony from the Trips. He's done their last three albums. All charted in Australia and the US. They've done big things for us." He talked softly and quickly. They had to lean forward to hear him.

"Phil says you're a pretty stable bunch. That's important. I don't want to know about bands that are gonna be screaming at each in six months. Anyway we've just signed the Zippers and we're touring them up the coast for two months. The thing is they need a support band."

He looked at them

"Touring's a good acid test for a young band. A bit make or break."

"He's asking us if we want to do it." Phil said unnecessarily.

Bonnie looked at the Martyr and then at Saul. She waited for him to express concerns about touring, about the studio, which studio, for how long, how much money on the tour, etc. She was ready to back him up with a sober face even though her blood and heart were kerjouncing. But he broke into a grin.

"Course we do."

He looked around.

"Don't we?"

The Martyr leaned back.

"Well, I'm not too busy for the next five years. I could zip up and down the coast with the Zippers."

Tony from Rubber Records left and they all huddled. Saul said don't get too excited yet. The Martyr said this is our last chance to change our name. What about Verso? Or Axis? Phil said Rubber were a small company but solid and had a reputation for nurturing bands. Saul said who wants to go drinking?

The Martyr said me.

Phil and Bonnie stayed at the table. She sensed something unfinished. Phil jingled his pockets nervously and looked at her.

"Tony wanted to know whether you were Saul's girlfriend or The Martyr's."

Her jaw clenched at the insult but she made herself speak lightly.

"Do you think it matters?"

"No, of course not."

But he jingled a bit more.

"Neither of them, actually. Haven't you noticed with those two? They don't have sex. They play guitars."

He didn't laugh.

"You know we'll have to start looking at clothes and other things."

"Absolutely."

"There's a certain image that we should aim for."

"And what's that?"

Anger gave her poise. Phil hedged. Tapped out a cigarette for her. Lit it.

"Well, while we're courting record companies it's probably best to stay on the conservative side. So things like —"

"What about the scruffy look that Tony was talking about?"

They looked at each other. Glasses rattled in a rack somewhere behind the bar.

"Record companies are easily frightened off. Bands can work for years perfecting their music but in the end it's the whim of the boys around some big table. They don't know about music. They know about money. They know about market. And they know about image. A scruffy look for women is not in."

"What do you have in mind for The Martyr and Saul? You going to get them to cut their hair?"

"I'm getting a drink. D'you want one?"

He bought two tequilas and pushed one across the table to her.

"A real drummer's drink, tequila. A band I managed in London were looking for a drummer once and it became a bit of a thing. They asked all the drummers who auditioned if they drank tequila. None of them knew if it would be a plus or a minus so they —"

"I'm not a big tequila drinker. Can't seem to get the taste for it."

Again their eyes locked.

"Maybe you could get used to it. For the band's sake."

"I don't think so."

"Maybe you could just pretend. Make believe you like it."

"I hate make believe. It smacks of lying."

Through the ice of anger Bonnie was enjoying this. She felt detached as she sometimes did after a gig. As though she were still up there.

"Before Firetown's second gig I was setting up my kit onstage and someone walked up and said 'when's the drummer getting here?' 'I am the drummer' I said. He just stared. I feel like a freak anyway. I might as well have the haircut too."

Phil shook his head.

"It won't matter what I wear. It's the way I play that counts."

"The first thing, the very first thing Tony asked me was, would she grow her hair? He didn't ask how long you'd been playing or how good you were."

"In my circles this haircut is quite normal"

He considered this while he chewed his lip.

"A lot of women come to see Firetown don't they?" he said eventually. As subtle as a crow diving for bread, she thought.

"Phil, I've got to go."

"Where are you going?"

"Celia's."

"Who's Celia?"

"She's a lesbian bar."

She passed her tequila over to him and stood up. He reached into his brief case and brought out a fistful of purple and green fliers. He offered them up to her, his face unreadable.

"Put these on the tables at Celia's. Would they let you do that? They're posters for Wednesday night."

"A manager to the end."

"Ah! But this isn't the end. This is just the beginning."

She took the posters, turned to leave and then turned to face him again.

"Do you think I'm a good drummer? You've never actually said so."

She didn't really care but it was their first real discussion and she was reluctant to leave it.

"Do you think I'd be sitting here sweating over your rugged good looks if you weren't? No! I'd be sitting here sweating about your replacement." He knocked back the tequila and stood. "Do you want a lift?"

"You knew all the time that I was a dyke didn't you?"

"I just wanted you to tell me in your own sweet way. I'm not a moron. I notice the women who come to see you play."

"You're a bastard."

"I know. But a dedicated one."

They shook hands. Somehow it seemed appropriate.

*

Bonnie ran down the lane behind Celia's. She was twenty minutes late even with the lift from Phil. Belle would be fine of course. She'd be sipping gin at the bar. She never danced; usually her outfit was too bulky, especially if she wore one of her capes. She was there to talk and be looked at.

A parked car up ahead of her shone metal and shadowed grey duco. There was a half moon high in the sky, which always made Bonnie think of Janis Joplin and now of course the song rose in her head.

Two men stood on the road in front of her. They glanced at her and then gave her their full attention. Ice stippled her scalp and her blood. They were probably harmless but her heart pounded now as she got closer. There was a bad feeling here but it was too late to turn around. Not too late, never too late, but her pride made her keep going. Jesus fuck them for screwing up women's lives. It was just around the corner for Christ's sake. Music seeped out through the cardboarded windows of Celia's.

"Is that her?"

"Yeah."

His voice familiar. It was the mixer, Glenn, with anger and excitement on his face.

"You smart arsed little bitch. You made me look like a fuckin' moron."

The car engine was tick ticking as it cooled. They must have followed Phil's car. She started backing away. There were pot holes behind her on the road. She felt her foot slip into one and saved herself from falling by stepping forward. The two men watched her.

"Not so fucking smart now are you?"

"Piss off. Leave me alone."

"I could play drums better with my dick."

"Look at the fuckin' haircut. Wanna be a bloke do ya?"

They spoke at the same time. The next minute she was screaming because she saw something in his hand and she turned and ran, her legs wheeling, blurring and her heart like an insistent knife in her chest. They didn't even chase her. They were too busy laughing.

*

"You have to charge them."

"No I don't."

She was sitting in Angela's lounge room with Belle next to her. Bonnie had run straight from the lane into a taxi and taken it to Angela's place which is where Belle had rung her, wondering where the hell she had got to. Classical music purred delicately in the background. This place is like an underground cavern where nothing can get in, thought Bonnie. She had knocked on Angela's door and when no-one answered rung her from a phone booth across the road. Angela had stood like a statue at the door while Bonnie swept past her sobbing. Angela had closed the door, chained it and then turned and looked at Bonnie. "What happened to your hair?" was the first thing she'd said.

"Shouldn't she, Angela?"

"Not if she doesn't want to."

"I think I want to go to bed," Bonnie said.

"Ring me if I can do anything."

"All right."

They listened for the sound of the ute. There it was. First gear, then up and into second gear, third gear and then there was nothing but the classical music again.

"Who is that?"

Its sweetness was piercing her.

"Mozart."

"Which one?"

"Piano Concerto in D minor."

They sat on the lounge and held hands and Bonnie thought, let's just stay plaited together like this. The scene in the lane played over and over in her head. She made up different endings. Good endings where she hit Glenn and he ran. And then bad endings where she was lying bleeding. She felt blood in her hair. The dull cut of a knife or the blunt explosion of wood on her skull. Then the scene started again. What had actually happened was getting duller and duller. It had been a grey sort of ending, except for the fan of purple and green paper on the road as she ran. Not really an ending at all. Angela rasped her hands through Bonnie's prickles.

"The contentious hair cut."

"I'm not going to grow it."

"Hmm."

'You think I should?"

"Yes."

"You've got short hair too."

"Bonnie you haven't got short hair. You've got a crewcut."

"Yes." She felt her head again, how soft it was. "It feels nice too."

"Bonnie, a crewcut is what men have. They walk into the barber and say I'll have a number two cut, thanks. God, if I had a crewcut like yours I'd be fired."

"My career's different."

"How is it different?"

"Rock music is … more broad minded."

"Is it? How far do you think you're going to get?"

"I don't want to lie about who I am. I've done that before."

A short silence.

"But you do realise that it wouldn't have happened if you'd kept your hair longer."

Bonnie was too tired to argue any more.

"I suppose not. And I suppose we have the right to wear our hair the way we want."

She put her hands on her knees to get herself into a standing position, looked at Angela and suddenly realised that she'd said something terribly wrong. Angela was glaring at her.

"Who's this 'we' you're talking about?"

"What?"

"I'm not a lesbian, Bonnie, if that's what you're implying. I'm bisexual."

"Fine."

"It's just sex, Bonnie. That's all it is. I don't belong in any feminist army."

They went to bed in silence. A short while later Bonnie felt the mattress sink and then lift as Angela got out of bed. Toilet, Bonnie thought and held off sleep until Angela came back. She wanted to put her arms around her and kiss her. But she fell asleep and dreamt that Phil had bought her a wig. Angela was in the dream as well. She was holding Bonnie down in the back lane behind Celia's and plastering the wig onto her head. She shouted something in Bonnie's ear but she couldn't understand it. Then the sentence became clear.

"Just wear it and you'll be famous. Just *wear* it."

The logic was firm and convincing. Bonnie woke up to weak daylight and the mutter of rain. She reached out, felt the huff of air beneath the sheet next to her and realised Angela had spent the night with Morgan.

They had a new mixer. His name was Jacob. "As in the Old Testament." He wore round glasses and had springy black hair. He shook her hand.

"Nice haircut you have there," he told her. "A bit long maybe."

"Jacob used to play guitar," Saul said. "Gave it up to be a mixer. Which is why he has loser written all over him."

"Mixing's more creative than people think. And people talk to me. I like that, as long as they don't spill anything on the desk. They buy me drinks too. What sort of side mix do you like?"

"Bit of bass drum, bit of snare, lots of bass guitar. Not too loud. I don't like to hear myself too much."

He nodded gravely.

"A fine blend."

Jacob was fast and efficient. He cleaned up the buzz that came out of the Martyr's effects pedals and tuned Bonnie's toms so that they were dry and deep. He had spare strings and spare picks.

"There's a lot of gaffer tape on your kit that doesn't really need to be there."

"Other engineers put it on when they're miking me up."

Jacob's face wrinkled with pain.

"Oh no. It makes it look ugly. The audience can't see it but you can and I can. I can get a great sound for you without all that tape flapping around. I promise."

"Now," he said when sound check was finished. "I want to work out some pre-show music. What would you like?"

Saul scritched his head and lifted one shoulder.

"Jacob, this isn't Les Girls. Play whatever you want."

"All right then." Jacob was unruffled. "How about Culture Club?" He tickled through a box of cassettes with two fingers. "Or Hayzee Fantayzee."

"They're crap. How about SPK?" The Martyr said.

"Perfect! Driving but harsh. And then the mellow but skilled sounds of you three."

The Martyr glared at Jacob, not sure if he was being sent up.

Jacob's glasses glinted at them from the back of the room all night. After the gig they bought him drinks at the Manzil Room. He pretended to suffer and sigh.

"Usually I don't drink," he said. 'But just for you lot I will."

Musicians came over to the table to talk about the state of music, the lack of good venues, how their band had nearly signed with a label last week but were beaten to it. One girl called Rosie sang in a band called Rust, who

97

Firetown had seen one night at The Britannia Hotel in Chippendale. Rust wanted to get a support with Firetown if that was possible, Rosie said. She clutched a demo tape, looking from Saul to The Martyr to Bonnie. She and Bonnie grinned at each other, female compatriots in a land of male players. Bonnie felt plain and ordinary next to Rosie. Her black hair was swirled and flared in homage to Siouxsie Sioux and she had cultivated the same pale face. She handed the cassette to Bonnie.

"Interesting haircut you've got," she told Bonnie.

"I was about to say the same to you."

The guitarist in Rust was her boyfriend, she explained. The drummer was her ex-boyfriend. But they all got on really well, she added quickly. Saul and The Martyr shuffled with embarrassment at the talk of relationships. Bonnie knew the Rust drummer. He was excellent. He wore a little black hat like a fez which was becoming his trademark and he had a strange dramatic way of plying his sticks, throwing his arms around. He would get noticed.

Rosie lit one cigarette from another then passed round the packet and left. As if people were waiting in line, the guitarist from Wrong Kind of Stone Age came to sit at their table and Saul and The Martyr talked to him in unusually matey tones while Bonnie sat in a contented silence. What a good life I have, she thought, what a bloody good life.

The Martyr ascended higher and higher in stoned splendour. He was drinking bourbon and smoked joints that he kept in rows in a tobacco tin. When he smoked, he forgot about his lisp. He waxed.

"Dictionaries should make reference to songs. They have origins of words. Y'know, Latin roots and stuff. They should have songs as well. For example I saw tupelo in the dictionary the other day. By accident. 'Tupelo,' it said, 'large North American swamp tree'. It should also say 'as referred to by Van Morrison in his famous song'."

"Lowlands," said Bonnie. "Land that is low lying. As in sad-eyed lady of."

The Martyr stared at her. "That's exactly what I mean." He turned to Saul. "She knows exactly what I mean."

"Have you eaten?" Bonnie asked him.

"Nah."

"I think you should."

"Do you?" he beamed at her. "Are you worried about me?" He looked at Jacob. "I have great drinking stamina. Excuse me, I'm going to throw up."

He disappeared beneath the table. Saul dropped a napkin down to him. Jacob watched the top of his head with interest.

"That's quite disgusting. Is he always like this?"

"Only when he's happy."

"Will they chuck us out?'

"We'll say he's looking for his keys."

"I suppose everyone vomits anyway. Look at Jimi Hendrix."

"Look at Brian Jones."

"He didn't vomit, he drowned."

"Look at Jim Morrison."

"Did Jim Morrison vomit?"

They talked like rock stars long into the night. Bonnie sat sleepily over her bourbon and held a picture of Angela's face in her mind.

6

Bonnie sat waiting for Charlie. The music shop had gone upmarket recently and sacrificed precious display space for a small waiting area with a coffee table covered in magazines. Steve Gadd was demonstrating stick techniques from a video screen in the corner. Two boys still in their school uniforms sat on the couch and watched with their mouths open.

"I could do that," one boy said. Gadd's arms were a blur. He was playing around a crescent of roto toms so fast that the beats merged one into the other.

"Yeah right," said the other. He picked up a copy of *Nightlife* magazine.

She felt the usual mild guilt that she felt before lessons these days. She hadn't practised much, had been playing a lot but not practising. Charlie gave her stern lectures about it.

"You might be playing lots of gigs but you still need to practise. What if you record soon? You need to have your technique perfect so that you don't stuff up. There's no room for time wasters in a studio."

She flipped through a *Modern Drummer.*

Beaty announce a new range of snare drums. Our guarantee of satisfaction warranty lets you take our snare home for 90 days. Drummers deserve the best. You decide! We guarantee your best playing time ever with Beaty snare drums. 5 x 14 or 6 x14 inch extra-strength, brass-plated snares.

There was an ad for autographed sticks imported from the US. Louis Bellson, Harvey Mason, Omar Hakim, Billy Cobham. She imagined her name embellished on drumsticks. Saw a stack of them in a special bin right next to the counter.

The two kids were snorting at something hilarious. They nudged each other and whispered. Barely.

"Ask her."

"No, you ask her."

The older boy leaned toward her.

"Hey! Can we have your autograph?"

"What?"

"You're famous."

"Yeah, we know your girlfriend."

They dropped the magazine onto the table and sat back to watch her. She picked it up.

Two pictures of Angela blazed from the cover. One was a publicity shot of her in a dazzling red dress, smiling. The other one showed her opening the door of her car. Bonnie stood on the passenger side in a tattered denim jacket. She was smiling over at Angela. The sky was leaden behind them and trees with bronze leaves framed the photo.

The headline above both photos read 'Angela Corbina's secret life'. And then in smaller letters 'Pics page 4'.

There were other headlines unrelated to Angela and Bonnie: *Wife tells of husband's secret sex orgies — I walked in on Ron and five others.*

The shark that ate two men — coastal town horror.

Bonnie drifted up to her feet, walked out of the shop, wandered along the street, the magazine heavy as wood in her fist. She was shaking as though chilled. Then she felt the yield of grass beneath her shoes and saw that she had stumbled into a park and that a group of old people were packing up a barbecue. They must be on an outing from somewhere, a nursing home or a hospital. A bus waited at the kerb for them while they walked backwards and forwards with thermoses, cushions.

Three women sat on a bench near Bonnie shrieking with laughter. A woman stood in front of them in a half crouch. She had dropped her walking stick on the ground and held a camera up to her face. Carefully she aimed. They waited. She aimed again, caution making her lose the moment.

"Come on, Myrt," one bench woman called.

"Wait on."

"We could die here."

"Here's as good as anywhere. All right." Myrt had it now. "Everybody say sex!"

"Sex!" they chorused. The camera clicked and they were released.

Bonnie sat on a bench and uncurled the magazine gingerly as though it had barely sheathed teeth. Page four was creased and ear marked at the corner.

SUNDAY LIVE *STAR IN LESBIAN ROMP!*

It seems that Angela Corbina has more on her mind than the renewal of her contract with the Eleven Network. Corbina, married to academic Morgan Fisher, was seen wining and dining this mystery woman during an afternoon's frolic. Angela may be married but she made no secret of her fondness for the girl in the denim jacket.

A picture of Bonnie and Angela brushing hands as they walked. A picture of Angela with Morgan, looking bored.

Sources at Eleven say that Corbina's contract for another series with Sunday Live *is by no means certain.*

The shiny paper hurt her eyes. There was more but she mashed the pages shut and then walked in a straight careful line to look for a phone booth.

*

101

Nora peered at the photo as though she had never seen Bonnie before.

"Why the hell didn't you tell me about her?"

"I couldn't."

"Did she tell you not to tell anyone?"

"Sort of."

"You shouldn't let anyone do that to you."

Bonnie looked at Nora levelly.

"You did it to me."

"So I did," Nora muttered.

"I'm going to call Angela from my mother's place."

"Why?"

"She's got a phone extension. Belle's going to give me moral support from the other phone."

"What are you going to say?"

"I'll tell her not to worry. That people will forget about it sooner or later. That I'm here if she needs me."

Nora threw her hands up in the air, palms up. It was the first time Bonnie had seen someone do it.

"Haven't you learnt anything from all this? She's not going to talk to you. You're a huge fucking threat to her career. You're a thorn in her side! She's had her fling, now she's getting ready to bail out."

Bonnie leaned over to pick up the copy of *Nightlife* that Nora had dropped.

"I don't know why people care that she sleeps with women."

"You're a bloody nutcase. What planet are you living on? Mars? This is a woman who goes everywhere with a male so that her cover isn't blown. Maybe in twenty years no-one'll care. But now ..."

"Yeah. Maybe in twenty years you won't be pushing your girlfriends onto the floor of your car."

"In twenty years Melanie and I'll be sipping gin and tonic on the verandah of a retirement village."

*

Clara wore a beige linen suit, as if the occasion called for something a bit dressy. She put water on for coffee and then perched on the edge of a big wooden dresser. Belle sat in the hallway next to the phone in a tiny chair and a black satin suit. She was dressed showily as well. Bonnie sat at the dining room table with the phone in her lap.

"Is this such a good idea, d'you think?" Clara asked.

"Sometimes lesbians have to make waves, Mrs Ransum."

Bonnie dialled Angela's number. The phone rang for a long time.

"Maybe she's out," Clara said.

"With all respect," Belle called out from the hall, "out is the last thing she is, Mrs Ransum."

"Belle, I wish you'd call me Clara."

"Sorry."

"Hello?"

A woman's voice.

"Angela?" Bonnie asked.

"One moment please."

Bonnie covered the mouthpiece. "She's got someone screening her calls."

Belle gently picked up the extension and held it next to her ear. Clara reached for Belle's packet of tobacco. From Angela's house came the sound of the phone being picked up from a table and a small, preparatory cough.

"You'll have to stop ringing, young lady."

It was Morgan's voice. Bonnie covered the phone again and whispered to her mother: "The flesh presser!"

"Who?" Clara asked.

"Her husband," Belle explained.

Bonnie said, "I'd like to speak to Angela, please."

"Angela's in no position to communicate with you. Surely you didn't expect that she would."

He didn't sound rattled. He was practically yawning. Bonnie looked at Belle. Belle raised a fist and frowned.

"I insist that I speak to her."

"Well, she's not here."

He sounded amused.

"Please ask her to call me."

"Don't beg!" Belle mouthed at her.

"She's just not interested, I'm afraid."

"Do you know who this is then?"

"Yes."

"When do you think Angela's going to admit to being a lesbian?"

Belle gave her a thumbs up.

"Pardon?"

"Are you happy that your wife sleeps with girls half her age?" Bonnie tried not to notice her mother rolling a thin anxious cigarette. Clara only smoked under extreme stress, or when she felt extraordinarily good.

"Now listen … " Morgan said.

"While you're in the house?" Bonnie asked. "Or may be you like that idea."

"I don't know what that magazine paid you but I'm happy to send you some sort of financial compensation, if it means that you won't disturb Angela. Or me."

Cold anger rinsed through Bonnie. "The question is ... what does she pay you to protect her?"

She hung up. Belle yipped with glee.

"What! What happened?"

"He was going to send me money!"

"You frightened the shit out of him!" Belle crowed.

"Did I? ... I don't know," Bonnie said. "I think he was just keeping up his end of an agreement."

She took the cigarette from her mother and felt the adrenalin drain away. The three of them reflected for a minute. Belle hadn't moved from the little wooden chair in the hall. Bonnie lit the cigarette and let it dangle from her fingers. She remembered the smell of Angela's neck and the steps leading up to the house on the first night they slept together. Angela had carried her into the house, fed her when she was hungry and given her gin when she was thirsty.

"Hey listen Bon." Belle said. "There'll be other women. Women who aren't scared of who they are."

"Darling, you're going to burn yourself."

Clara took the cigarette from Bonnie and crushed it into an ashtray, mashing it long after the red glow had died.

*

Bonnie started the long, weighing-up of a good thing gone bad. She lay on her bed and looked at her hands. Calluses had formed on her fingers in the places where painful blisters had opened, closed and re-opened. Her hands had played on even when they bled and now she had toughened skin. Loyal hands. Hardworking hands.

It was her brain that was the problem. She would have to think more in future. Her mind ticked over as cold as a watch while she wondered at how she'd seen this improbable adventure as love. Angela probably spent the last ten years replacing Jude with various women. It chilled her to remember the frank and touching admission that first day in bed: "You look like her. You have her face."

Lots of things stood out in a harsh light. It was as though she was standing in a house whose floorboards had been rotting for years and now she could see right through to pure, plain dirt. She finally understood the groaning of old timber.

There had been another article in *Nightlife*. They'd run a photo from the Queensland tour. There were the five actors, three men and two women, just as Angela had described. They had their arms around each other, something the text didn't neglect to mention. Agnes Anne had written the article. She promised a follow-up story in the next issue. Agnes Anne. What sort of name was that?

Bonnie examined the photo until it collapsed into dots. She kept the article on her bed for days. She woke up some mornings to find it digging into her side. She read it again and again. Bonnie did look like Jude. They might have been twins. The same eager parenthesis of cheeks, the same trusting smile. She would have faced life easily. She would have grabbed it.

*

Belle had found work in Perth for twelve months. She was apologetic when she told Bonnie at Celia's Bar. Smoke swirled from a fan above them as they leaned towards each other. Bass-rich music chugged like machinery from speakers clamped to the ceiling.

"I feel like I've dropped you in it somehow," she shouted, yelling into Bonnie's ear. "This whole mess."

"I dropped myself in it."

"Hey listen, keep my car until I come back OK?"

"Thanks."

"That way you can get out of trouble faster."

They toasted each other with shots of brandy and on Sunday Bonnie drove Belle to the airport. At the departure gate they hugged and then had a last look at each other. Belle looked oddly wide-eyed and owlish.

"My eyes hurt," she smeared at them with her knuckles. "I feel like I might cry."

Bonnie tried to feel like she might cry as well but she didn't.

"Good luck Belle."

"Are you all right?"

"Yep. Ring me soon."

She tipped back on her heels one last time and then Belle disappeared down the corridor behind a man and his complaining child. Bonnie turned around and started to walk.

"Good morning and welcome back to *Sunday Live.*"

She lifted her head up to where the voice came from and saw Angela's face suspended from the ceiling, her eyes sparkling, her hair grown out and carefully brushed to the side. From televisions around the airport lounge Angela smiled down at her.

She has the look of straight women who are protected. Who had said that about Angela? Bonnie tried to remember as she walked onto the walkway, down the escalator and into the carpark. She reached Belle's ute, leaned against it and fumbled for the cigarette packet. An Ansett plane lifted and bisected the blue patch above her. Then she remembered that Belle had said it. Bonnie raised a hand to the sky and waved.

*

On the tenth of June she got a reminder call from Jacob that Firetown were playing at the Trade Union Club that night. She hadn't picked up her sticks since the day she read *Nightlife*. Now she sat behind her rubber practice kit and propped a page of rudiments on the music stand. She would get herself up to speed. But her wrists were awkward and angled. Her rolls were irregular like a beginner's. She stopped and breathed for a while.

"All right," she told herself. "get it together. Feel it."

She said it aloud as though Charlie were there saying it. She played some time on her own and then played to music. Playing to music was all right but it didn't flow. It followed tamely.

Round wooden tables, chairs still upended on most of them, were scattered around the third floor of the Trade Union Club. Firetown sat in various postures, on bar stools, table edges. They straightened up when she walked out of the creaking lift.

Her kit was onstage waiting for her with a lone spotlight on it as though it was the star act. She ran a hand across the silky red wood. Jacob hopped up with an armful of mikes while she was tilting her toms for easier reach.

"Did you notice these?" he said.

Delicate microphone clamps flowered from the rims of her drums. She hadn't noticed.

"Tiny, aren't they? They're really strong and they won't get in your way either. And look." He jiggled one loose and it sat in his hand like a small plastic spider. "You can move them around easily. They bend here at this flex stem so I can attach them at any point on the drum."

"They're great."

He attached mikes to the spiders, worked his way around the kit. He sang something to himself in a comforting hum. 'Mantelpiece', it sounded like. Saul came and stood at the foot of the stage. She could sense disapproval coming from him in waves.

"Everything OK?" she asked.

"Sure."

He wandered away. Jacob's voice came up from her bass drum.

"Looks like I'll have to tell you. That guy Tony from Rubber Records isn't interested in Firetown any more."

She went cold.

"Anything else?"

Jacob stood up.

"Saul says maybe you should grow your hair."

They played three songs to check the levels. 'The Heart of It', 'The Attack', 'Life Number Two'. Her awkward wrists stayed on the ends of her arms. Her drumming was mechanical and wooden. Lead in her arms slowed her. The Martyr and Saul looked at each other and then away.

"Is your mix all right?" Jacob yelled from the desk. She nodded.

"Let's do 'Mantelpiece'."

Things improved. Jacob pumped more bass guitar through her foldback just in case and it helped. After the sound check they sat together and had a drink. A man behind the bar was unloading bottles of Scotch from a case stamped 'fragile'. Phil gave an introductory cough. Firetown looked at him.

"Listen, Tony isn't interested any more. We know why, I think. That thing in *Nightlife* about Bonnie."

Thing.

"But we'll soldier on OK? It doesn't matter. It may win us some new fans."

"How?"

"People will come to see us."

She looked blank.

"Didn't you read the article?"

"No, not the first one."

She had read bits. The introduction. She saw the photos. That was enough. Phil looked stumped.

"Well, it mentioned that you were a drummer. A woman drummer. Not many of you around."

"I feel like a performing monkey."

Jacob shook his head.

"Just forget all this shit. Forget it." He waved a hand. "It's gone. Just play."

He was right of course. Just *play*. Dykes came to see the band because of her anyway. She knew that. No big difference that it had been made official by *Nightlife*. Play. That is, if she could play still, through this blinding sense of loss, followed by surges of love for Angela. And then more loss. Like a big rip in her heart.

She looked up. Saul had gone off to ring someone. He was curved around the phone at the end of the bar. The Martyr was stuffing tiny head phones into his ears with an air of concentration. Was this going to be the entire conversation about their lesbian drummer?

They weren't interested in anything about her, she knew that now. Saul was driven by one thing only — the desire to succeed. Everything else was measured against it. He didn't care about her, unless she stood between him and his goal. The Martyr didn't care as long as he could play guitar with Saul.

She sat at the table, which kept shifting and rocking on a triad of uneven legs. Her fingers were still and quiet. The tight little group was disintegrating.

*

She played badly.

"So you had an off night. So what?" Jacob shrugged. She had come to him for solace.

"I stuffed up too," the Martyr said. "In 'Round and Round'. Did you hear it?" He snapped a beer can open.

Saul nodded. "Yeah. I heard you."

"Played a fucking great A chord instead of an E. Fuck!"

He rinsed beer around his teeth.

The next day she sat at the practice kit and worked at it with teeth clenched. Something refused to give. That night she walked through Darlinghurst with Nora and listened for rhythms but her normally restless jaw refused to yield them up.

"Hey!" Nora was shaking her shoulder suddenly.

"Sorry."

"Did you hear it?"

"What?"

"This question I heard a psychologist ask on TV. See what *you* come up with: 'You're twenty-four. What do you know for sure?'"

Bonnie considered the question. I know I miss Angela. I know for sure I can't play drums for shit. She went cold with panic. Firetown had another gig on Friday.

*

People were calling out for them to start. Firetown walked onstage and the mutter of conversation grew into a roar. When Bonnie tried to focus on a few faces the light blinded her. Two of the lights clamped onto the lighting tree at the right of the stage threw a fiery caste onto everything and made Firetown glow. Bonnie felt like an army of one with severe battle nerves. She was preparing for a battle with the Thing in her that wasn't playing any more. She checked the list at her feet which was written carefully in Saul's black texta.

<u>Set One</u>
Smoke and Mirrors
Life Number Two
Clown School
How the World Works

Saul gestured to Jacob at the desk. Jacob gave a thumbs up and Saul stepped back into the dark to check his tuning again. His strings scratched. The needle on his tuner waved crazily. The Martyr was pacing around saying **bub**ada**bub**ada**bub**ada to himself. And Phil was practically wringing his hands off from his position on the side of the stage.

Sweat damped her hands and sticks. She bowed her head as if praying. The song faded. She clicked in 'Smokes and Mirrors'. It was hard work but the first song of the night was always a strain, like a cold engine coughing awake. The band hadn't warmed up and anyway instrumentals were always hard, with nowhere for an audience to focus but the blur of strings and chop of the beat. No words to detract from their playing. Every time she lifted her stick she had to think about when she was going to put it down again. Lift, drop. Lift, drop. For the first time ever she dreaded playing fills around the kit.

She was going to fall off the cliff.

But didn't.

The crowd yelped at the end of each song. A small knot of dancers at the front helped. They swooped down to 'Repeat and Forget' and as soon as the lights went down onstage she darted off and walked to the bar. Got herself lost among people. A hand clamped onto her arm.

"Excuse me? Great playing."

"Thanks."

"I appreciate good craft. In any area."

The woman flounced a hand through her shoulder length hair. Bonnie wasn't sure what her response should be. She became aware of the sweaty singlet she had on.

"Yeah?"

"Do you want a drink?" the woman asked.

"Yes thanks. Bourbon and coke."

"You drink Coke for energy I suppose. You must lose a lot of fluid up there. Do you have water next to you when you play?"

Her voice was a sort of purr. She sounded like she really wanted to know. She signalled to the barman and ordered. A patina of smoothness shone from her. Bonnie got the feeling she was an expert in some area and had come here to escape for a while and fill her brain with sound waves. She wasn't a rock 'n roll kind of person. Anyone could tell that by her dress. More an academic type. Fortyish.

"Is it hard?"

"Is what hard?"

Bonnie was handed her drink.

"Playing the drums."

Tonight it is, she was tempted to say.

"Sometimes. If there are emotional upheavals in my life for instance."

"That's interesting," the woman said. And she sounded interested.

"I suppose it's like anything creative," Bonnie said.

How pretentious! It was what Belle might have said. But the woman accepted this remark. Bonnie imagined herself living with this academic in a small house. Booklined rooms, fireplace, quiet nights reading. No loud music. No rehearsals. Biscuits in a tin. Coffee on a tray. No whirring fridge. No noise, no smoke. She swallowed the drink. Ice cubes singed her teeth.

"But I can tell that you don't know much about drumming."

"Why?"

The woman was not offended or surprised. Bonnie tapped out two cigarettes from the pack and offered one. The woman ignored the offer.

"My playing's shithouse tonight."

"Are you upset about something?"

Bonnie lit up.

"I don't know. I can't *feel* anything somehow. Maybe it's something else."

Another clinical, interested nod from the woman. Saul appeared at her elbow. His long hair flicked around his neck as he turned and looked at the woman. He was scowling. What's going on, Bonnie wondered, and then realised. *He thinks I've picked her up.*

"We have to go on again."

"See you later."

The woman nodded.

She finished her cigarette and squashed it into an empty glass backstage before climbing up the tiny steps. She felt soothed and cared for as if she'd just been to the doctor. She played well for 'The Attack' and then lost it again so that 'The Heart of It' lumbered like a sleepy bear. She dropped a stick onto the floor tom. Looked for the woman but couldn't see her. Her eyes settled on Jacob at the mixing desk and there she was! Holding one drink, putting one down for him. Very carefully. And then leaning over, shouting into his ear. Friends maybe. And then the red light blinded her and they were swallowed up in darkness.

She played now as though it was a typewriter in front of her, not a semi-circle of drums. Stolidly, as though waiting for five o'clock. 'Speechless',

'Round and Round'. The Martyr was facing front while Saul walked backwards and forwards between her anxious face and the front row to check on her progress. They had planned 'Mantelpiece' for the encore song. Firetown waited gravely for the applause, thirty seconds of clapping, and then launched into it.

It was working, but then 'Mantelpiece' always did. It was a fantastic song. The drums were holding up everything. Leading the way. Little streamers of bass clung to each punch of snare drum. Good work Bonnie, she told herself. You didn't fall. Not once.

"Let's do 'The Heart of It' again!" Saul shouted to her. She clicked it in. She was swimming now.

She forgot her playing and let the song play itself, no longer tied to each lift and fall of her left hand. And then panicked. How many verses had they played? Two or three? Shit! She guessed that they had played three and slowed down to end the song but Saul and The Martyr played on to the third verse. She started up again but the hole was there. A big gaping chasm. She had fallen for the first time.

"Sorry," she said in the dressing room. "Sorry sorry."

Phil hardly noticed. "Can we talk for a minute? Have a band meeting?"

"OK."

"Have a beer," Phil said and handed them around.

When she sensed he was mollycoddling, everything went into slow motion. She would swear to improve. She would practise for days, not sleep. She would develop a winning edge. She'd say, I know my playing's been shit lately because of ... well you know ... but that's all finished with. The Martyr and Saul looked at the floor.

"That guy from Rubber Records rang Saul and me today," Phil said.

"Tony."

"Yes, Tony. He's still interested in the band. He thinks the lesbian thing is a problem though."

She clutched at the slippery cold glass as though it would keep her up.

"The lesbian thing! I thought we'd talked about that. You said we'd soldier on and that —"

"He's offered us a contract. But they want you to look different."

The Martyr said, "How?"

"Can't you imagine?" Bonnie asked him. "They want a Tina Weymouth."

Her crewcut was suddenly a battle helmet, her singlet a banner of protest.

"I'm not changing the way I look."

Silence.

"I'm not."

"We can work it out. It's not too much of a problem, is it?" The Martyr asked. Saul's gaze was still fixed on the floor.

"They're not saying 'don't sleep with women'. They're saying be discreet."

"I'm sick of discreet. I'm not hiding anything and I'm not going to play in a fucking dress."

"Not a *dress* exactly."

"What then?"

Phil said nothing. He didn't know what it was Rubber Records wanted, she realised. But she did. What they wanted was to change her essence.

She walked outside and looked for Jacob. He was rolling up leads, a ball of used gaffer tape stuck to his shirt.

"There you are ! Listen there was a woman talking to me tonight," he said.

"I know! I was going to ask you —"

"Agnes Anne."

She searched her mind. Found the connection.

"Shit!"

"Wanted to know about you. I started chatting away then I got suspicious. I thought, 'who's this glamour doll?' She started asking about … you know," he ducked his head as though Angela was hidden below the floorboards, "… her. She wasn't going to say who she was but eventually she said, 'I'm Agnes Anne'. She didn't mention *Nightlife*. But I did. I told her to leave you alone. Then I told her to leave. 'I don't think so, I'm a paying customer', she says. Like anyone else here. 'No, you're not I said. You're here to snoop'."

It was like listening to film dialogue.

"'Why don't you piss off?' I said. She took it really calmly. I reckon it's not the first time someone's said that to her."

Jacob angry. She'd never seen him like this. His fingers clenched and straightened, clenched and straightened. He pushed his glasses firmly back between his eyes. The crowd drained out through the exit. She and Jacob got some sidelong glances.

"Listen, I'm leaving."

"Yeah, she might still be lurking. I'll take down your kit."

"No no. I'm leaving the *band.*"

"Why?"

He stood with one hand outstretched at the end of a loop of cable. He hadn't been told anything.

"They want a straight drummer."

"Who does?"

"Rubber Records."

She thought he would be shocked but he kept rolling lead.

"It's not a huge surprise, I suppose. Phil and Saul are ruthless. Saul's smelt the contract and he's chasing it. Martin's just a door mat. Of course you have to leave. But there's plenty of other bands around. I know one or two bands looking for a drummer."

"I'm quitting playing."

Hadn't known it till this second but if her playing had slipped because of Angela, now it would abandon her altogether, like a tin roof sheering off in a storm.

"You might for a while but you'll come back to it."

She had heard that somewhere. She had said it to Saul one night at the bank. Saul, who had hung his head tonight and not said a word.

"Can I talk you out of it?"

She shook her head.

"This business is ..."

"You're doing the wrong thing," Jacob said.

There was suddenly a silence. A musicless silence. Was she really doing the wrong thing? She opened her mouth to ask him for the other bands' numbers.

"But God, what do I know?" he said.

"Your tape's stopped."

They heard the call for last drinks.

7

Bonnie became inordinately fond of smoking. She wished Belle could see her sitting back in her chair with her feet on the desk. Tilting her head back. Inhaling. Her hand hovering six inches in front of her face. Two seconds and then sighing it out as if it was a relief to be rid of the fumes. Traffic flowed away down the hill outside her window and books littered her desk. *Australian Towns. Our Early Settlers. Aboriginal Place Names. Cities in the Dust.*

She was on assignment for a friend of Melanie's called Anne. They'd met in potting class but Anne gave up potting to publish Australian experimental poetry. She thought there may be money in it. She had gone broke. Lost most of her life savings. But she had another idea now and wanted someone to help her research it.

She invited Bonnie over to her house and they sat in the pocket hanky garden. There were sad baskets of geranium. Impatiens flourished in damp corners green with mould. Anne's girlfriend had left her not long ago, Anne said, after she had lost her money. She had been the gardener, not Anne, so now plants were running a bit wild. A bird feeder full of water dripped sadly, and a pot of tea skidded around a rickety wrought iron table. They held their cups in their hands.

Anne hung onto the disaster of the poetry. It gnawed at her.

"I printed two thousand copies of each collection. Two thousand!"

Bonnie wondered if that was a lot, or not enough.

"I was lucky to sell fifty."

"Golly."

"Have you ever bought a book of poetry, Bonnie?"

"I bought the collected works of Dylan once. Second hand."

"Yes well. Look at him. What an irony. A genius dead at thirty nine."

Bonnie saw their crossed paths but stayed silent. She wondered if there was milk for the tea.

"Poetry's dead." Dismissed with a hand. "No-one reads it. No-one buys it. So I thought about tourists and what they might like to read. They'd need a quick read. On the bus going to the Opera House. On the ferry going to Manly. Lists are what they'd like."

"Lists?"

"Yep." She leaned back and steepled her fingers. "So I compiled a list of the birds and flowers they're likely to see near tourist spots. Seagulls and petrels on the harbour. Magpies at the NSW Art Gallery. Lorikeets, black cockatoos and king parrots up at Katoomba. Blue gums and black boys in

— anyway you see my point. I put a little box next to the bird or plant so that they could tick them off as they spotted them. I left copies in all the shops around the tourist spots. And they loved it! German and Danish tourists were carrying them everywhere. Spent hours wandering around outside of the Art Gallery apparently. Some of them didn't even go in!"

She sipped her tea and savoured the best part. The golden moral of the tale.

"They sold out in a month. I'm up to my third edition."

"Wow."

"So now I'm thinking of lists of small towns. It would encourage tourists to hire cars. I could get sponsorship from a car rental company to cover print costs. Also, they'd drive right into the Australian outback. Really get to the heart of it, not just wander around the edges. And then I could have the same box for them to tick and descriptions of the town. Population, type of birds, type of trees. That sort of thing."

"Australia-wide?"

"Australia-wide … hmm."

It seemed Anne hadn't considered leaving New South Wales but Bonnie now held the whole continent out to her temptingly.

"Yes. Yes. Why the hell not?" She shook her head. "God you'll have your work cut out."

So Bonnie smoked and read reference books. Nollatud, Deehi, Bangalong, Whelpa, Burrburra, Whipaki. Population 60,000. Population 32,000. Only the most unusual names, Anne had said. She compiled a list of questions for Anne each week.

"Do you want cattle mentioned? Sheep? How many there are in each town?"

"Whoa! Hang on."

Silence at the other end.

"Well. Maybe mention the primary industry in each town."

"What about actual town size in hectares?"

"All right."

It was amazing how little she had thought the list through. Bonnie persevered. Noises from the flats around her were now an irritation. The irregular rhythms of activities drove her to go out and look for a quieter place. She made an excursion of it and drove out of Darlinghurst heading west with all her books piled in Belle's car. She drove up Parramatta Road and then swung off the highway to drive down streets where old street lamps still hung by wires down the centre of the road. There were gardens full of hydrangeas that half hid the Federation houses behind them. She eventually found a library next to a small park. Two girls screeked on rusty swings. A woman sat on a bench watching them.

"Push us, Mum." The mother stood wearily, pushed her cardigan sleeves up and the little girls shrieked with the excitement to come.

Bonnie toiled up the stairs, her arms full of books, and pushed the glass doors open with her foot. A librarian at the counter with straight hair brown as river water glanced at her, looked down at the book she was covering in plastic then glanced again at Bonnie.

"These are borrowed from other libraries. Is that all right?" Bonnie asked. She could barely see the woman over the stack.

"That's fine."

"What suburb is this by the way?"

The librarian blinked. "Ashfield."

She sat at a table where she could look out over a cluster of trees in the park. Old men sat in thick plastic chairs and dozed. They had no books in front of them. They were just coming in out of the May cold. They didn't even pretend to read. The library was warm and quiet. There were no earnest students rummaging through the shelves, no noisy photocopier. The borrowers were retired people who scanned the large print section slowly and thoroughly. The checkout beep at the counter was comforting, not intrusive. Bonnie felt on the verge of sleep. She put her head down on her arms and dozed. She woke up, scrubbed at her face with her hand, and got to work again. In her notebook she found a recent postcard from Belle and read it again.

Weather extremely hot. It never rains here. Fremantle is a fantastic place. Have met a woman called Hilary who writes poetry. Poetry! Imagine me with a poet. Bonnie couldn't. She likes my cape. When are you coming to visit? I've got lots of room. The house has polished floorboards and a view of the ocean.

Old men snored gently. Bonnie worked on through the outback of Queensland. Tiny populations, huge numbers of cattle. She worked for three solid hours and decided to make the library a regular work place. She came back every third day or so, the pile of books under her arms changing.

Two children came in to the library every time Bonnie was there. They talked in ridiculous stage whispers. One afternoon, the girl dropped a pile of picture books she was carrying, just as she had reached her seat in the kids section. The books exploded and scattered on the lino and old men jumped and moaned in their seats.

"Listen you two!" the librarian said, suddenly fierce. "Keep it down or out you go."

The children sshhed each other.

*

116

Nora and Melanie took Bonnie to the movies one Saturday.

"Just remember when we leave halfway through that it wasn't my choice," said Melanie.

The film was about a singer called Angel who worked as a waitress. A record executive heard her singing while she washed dishes and signed her up right there in the kitchen. She became a star. This was demonstrated by the flowers that lined the dressing room and the men who appeared suddenly to give them to her. Angel's record went top ten, surprise surprise.

"Baby, this is just the beginning." her manager said.

Bonnie sat in the dark and wondered how Firetown were. She hadn't been out to see a single band since she stopped drumming. Maybe Firetown weren't playing any more. Maybe, she hoped, they folded.

"Predictable or what." Melanie scraped the bottom of the popcorn container. "The fame, the drug problem, the dirt-poor family. That nice barman. All morals, no ambition." she found some crumbs. "He'll rescue her for sure."

Bonnie dreaded seeing the band making it, but the musicians were kept in the background while Angel's dramas unfurled drearily. She fell in love with the strong, silent guitarist. Bonnie imagined the lisping Martyr in the role. The drummer and bass player didn't even get a speaking part.

"Long live the melody makers for they are the kings," she muttered.

"Stop being jealous," Nora told her.

"Oh God, now she's pregnant!" said Melanie disgustedly.

*

One afternoon the boy brought in some coffee in a take-away foam cup. He walked like a sleepwalker, as though the coffee was brimming in his own bare, cupped hands, and lowered it inch by inch next to the returns slot. The librarian was on the phone. He did a little hopping dance of anticipation from foot to foot. He looked around and saw Bonnie watching him. He immediately stopped his dance. The librarian got off the phone and exclaimed at the coffee. She admired the wooden stirring paddle and the two sachets of sugar. She kissed him extravagantly.

So she was their mother! Bonnie couldn't believe she hadn't realised this before. The embrace was intimate and loving. Of course now she thought about it the boy's hair was identical to the librarian's — brown as healthy wholesome dirt, smooth as silk but in his case, cut very short. He was ten or eleven with big sticking-out ears.

The boy stood sated by his mother; fed by her. He was grinning hugely with his satchel still on his back, too young to need to reject his mother's love. Bonnie looked away and something grieved inside. Something lurched.

She looked back down at her small towns of Australia. Pocato, Lesting, Wafer. She imagined the large rivers running through them. Willow trees. Tyres hanging from ropes. There was another question for Anne. She leaned busily over her notebook. Rivers? she jotted. Length? Width?

Later the librarian passed by her table and glanced at the mess of pages. "What are you working on?"

"A book."

The librarian took a seat with the surprise of it.

"I thought it was just some long assignment. So where's it set? You must be researching it like crazy."

"It's not fiction. It's a reference book for tourists."

The librarian was clearly disappointed. She stood up. Bonnie felt driven to a defence of Anne's project and described the first book of lists in detail. The tourists wandering around the Domain, ticking in boxes. Black cockatoos in Katoomba. The librarian sat back down again. Then Bonnie painted a glamorous picture of the second book — days on the road, outback life, small hotels, wide brown rivers. More boxes ticked.

"So that tourists can get to the heart of the country," she trailed off.

Old men snored in their chairs like distant speedboats.

The librarian looked sceptical. "This rehashing of old material," she said, shaking her head. "It's as bad as television. No new ideas, just combinations of old ones."

Television! Bonnie's eyes dulled. Memories of Angela. A shirt that strobed. Breasts. Blackheath corridors. Six Angelas smiling at her from the departure lounge. The librarian noticed the blurred look on her face.

"I'm sorry! I didn't mean to offend you. I'm sure it's a great project."

Bonnie scratched her arm and knocked a book to the floor. "It's OK. I'm not offended."

She went back to work but a minute later needed to get out and have a cigarette. Over at the park she sat on a bench near the swings. Dry leaves skittled in whorls around her. There were curls of heavy purple cloud in the eastern sky. There was rain ahead. Maybe a storm. She remembered Angela's forecasting.

"Come on, do your worst," she told the sky. Then she played her oldest game. If the sky cleared, something fantastic would happen to her in the next seven days. She lit up again and waited, cupping the cigarette inside her curled hand like a tough guy. Rain drops drifted down gently as snow.

*

The librarian was in a mood. She banged books around and her long hair trailed behind her in a wrathful wake. Her anger had surfaced after a phone call. She hadn't raised her voice but her fingers drummed the table. Readers kept their eyes on their books but listened meekly. Bonnie watched her pacing from the corner of her eye. Maybe there was something she could say to cheer her up. But she thought of nothing.

She went out and sat on the library steps to smoke a cigarette. Mothers and their children did the rounds of the park – two swings, a strange row of hand rings and a roundabout. What a dreary bloody life. But then what was so great about her own life? Not a single rhythm tremored through her. Her body was in storage, waiting for winter to be over. She drew on her cigarette and imagined the park covered in snow, ice shimmering on the chains and slides. There was the sound of tongue clicking coming from above her left shoulder.

"D'you want emphysema like all the men in there?" It was the librarian, looking down at her sadly. "Haven't you heard them coughing their guts out?"

Bonnie leapt to her feet, hunting for something to say in defence of smoking. And found not a single one, except the occupation of hands and mouth. The librarian walked inside, her brown hair tossing backwards and forwards before disappearing altogether. It had been a swoop attack and Bonnie had been napping as usual.

*

"Are you seeing someone, Mum?"

Her mother sounded different to Bonnie. Her voice was lighter, her tone more dramatic than usual.

"What gave you that idea?" Clara's voice like a little lark, trilling up and down.

"You haven't called much." Tried not to sound petulant.

"I know …"

There was a significant pause which Bonnie didn't end. They had hardly spoken since the Angela incident. Bonnie was concerned that she had put her mother off any experiments she might have been considering.

"Yes, I am. Well, not really 'seeing' …"

"Who is he? What's his name?"

"Ben."

"Ben." A young name.

"Yes."

"I'll have to meet him."

"He's very nice. He's an architect. And he has no children."

Obviously a plus for Clara who had been through all that.

"Be nothing worse than to shack up with someone with kids."

"Anyway, Bonnie, come over soon. We'll go out for dinner."

119

"All right."

"How's the list?"

Her mother was the only person proud of this career change. Bonnie didn't mention Anne's vague steering of the whole book project, the fact that it was a one person company teetering and skidding like her teapot on the table.

"Fine. I'm in South Australia now."

"You'd better watch out for dust storms."

They had a little laugh at that and then hung up. Her mother was not going to experiment with a female lover. She imagined asking her mother the question that Nora had asked her.

"Mum, you're forty-eight. What do you know for sure?"

Clara would say, "Well, I know for sure that I'm not getting any younger. I know for sure I'll never find the woman who liked straw hats."

Her mother with an architect, Belle with a poet. Bonnie with books on Australia up to her ears. She could reel off the names of towns around the country but still had no map of her life.

8

Two days later when she walked into the library a woman was sitting on a small portable stage reading aloud. She was practically shouting. A group of pensioners sat watching her intently. The regulars observed from their plastic armchairs. No-one was asleep. There was hardly a spare chair in the place.

The librarian came up to Bonnie, who stood cradling her usual ridiculous load.

"Sorry, I should have warned you. The first Thursday of every month we have a book reading for senior citizens."

Bonnie was flattered. Why should she be warned?

"Don't worry. I'll come back later."

"Why don't you come out the back and work? There's coffee. There's a desk. This place'll be empty again in an hour."

"All right."

They tiptoed across the floor. The old people were rapt in the story, standing on the pitching deck of a ship where a white-haired captain shouted at his first mate. Mutiny or a bad storm brewed on the pages ahead. Their eyes flicked to the librarian and Bonnie, then shifted back to the reader.

The librarian opened a door, closed it and the reading voice faded. The back room was dingy; peeling walls were made worse by an attempt at decoration. Posters everywhere exhorted people to read more books. Why were they hung out here where no-one could see them? A photo board covered with pictures hung slightly askew.

Bonnie sat at the desk and looked at the little scenes while the librarian thrust a cord in a plastic jug. There was the boy who had carried in the coffee. And the girl next to him in a pink dress with white lace frosting, seven or eight years old, with her mother's straight hair. Both of them had their arms tight around the librarian, one on either side, as if she was a lifeline.

"My kids. Obviously."

"Yeah, I've seen them."

"I try to get them to go to my sister's after school but for some reason they want to come here."

Bonnie looked at her. The woman didn't know that her kids adored her.

"Why wouldn't they want to?"

"Well, libraries can't be so great for kids when they've read every book ten times. I don't have the money to replace them either. The books I mean." She gave a wry smile. "There's cake here of some sort."

She took half a brown, sugared ring out of a box. She had enormous hands, Bonnie noticed.

"Do you live around here?" she asked Bonnie.

"Darlinghurst."

"You drive all the way here from Darlinghurst? Milk?"

"Yeah. Yeah."

The librarian put the cup and cake on the desk.

"Thanks."

Bonnie stacked her books on the desk in order of size. Large, then small, then pocket book. A pyramid. Then changed them around and started with colour large, colour small, black and white large, black and white small. They towered in the unsteady pile, ready to topple.

The librarian watched with interest.

"What are you doing?"

"Playing."

The librarian made herself a coffee and then went, leaving Bonnie with her arranging. In the time the door took to wheeze shut behind her, Bonnie heard a woman outside say: "You know, I never open a book without learning something new."

*

The girl and boy sat as close as empty brackets at one of the low tables. They were prowling through a big picture book. Bonnie settled near the biographies and watched them. Every now and then they glanced up and located their mother. Reassured they continued their silent reading.

"Turn," the girl said in a blank voice. The boy turned the page. Silence, a quick glance at their mother and then, "turn".

Turn, read, glance up, turn. Bonnie hoped their weekends were more exciting than this. The library was busy today. The librarian was shouting at an ancient woman at the counter.

"No! It's not in yet!"

"Eh?"

The woman's transparent raincoat enfolded a wizened stick of body. There was a glimpse of flowered smock. Her right arm came up like a salute to curl her ear forward. She was keen to hear about this, her reading matter.

"Next week!!"

"?"

"Next week!!"

An old man near Bonnie sighed but he was asleep and not listening. The librarian showed not a scrap of impatience, she didn't roll her eyes at the next person in the queue who stood amused and ready to be an accomplice.

"Next week?" The woman had heard now.

"Yes! I'll put it aside."

She made a motion with her hands of placing something on her left. The children looked down again.

"Turn."

The woman nodded.

And so on to the next problem.

Bonnie had listed 34 towns from South Australia. She thought that was too many. Jotted a question for Anne in her notebook, "how many per state?", knowing already that Anne would not have thought about it.

She would do the Northern Territory next. The Top End. She imagined the towns there; the names a symbol of their eccentricity. Big trucks that rolled in and unloaded vegetables and frozen chickens. The European tourists could sit at the cafes and tick boxes while the flies teased their ears.

That was all for today. She had a coffee craving. The librarian was still stamping books with a chonking sound.

"See you later." Bonnie put her back against the glass door to push herself out.

"I didn't ever tell you, did I?" the librarian said as she picked up another book. She didn't look up from her work, so it wasn't clear who she was talking to. The sleeves of her white shirt were rolled up to the elbow but kept coming down to dangle at her wrists.

Slide, chonk, slide. Bonnie hesitated. Was she talking to her? She walked back inside the library and stood waiting.

"Tell me what?"

"What I'm working on."

"No."

Bonnie juddered her left boot very loudly across the lino but the librarian went on calmly.

"Librarians are a bit like teachers. That's the popular image, I think. Failed at one thing so they do something else. Except librarians are often moving on to something else in their life." She pushed her cuffs back up to her elbows. "Working in libraries is just a step on the way."

She seemed to be addressing not just Bonnie but the queue of women with their books waiting to be chonked. Some of them nodded as if they too were on their way to somewhere great and significant.

"I'm working on Gail."

"Who's Gail?"

"Gale," the librarian looked up at Bonnie, "is the Great Australian Lesbian Epic."

The line of pensioners swept their heads sideways to look at the librarian. There was a hush as the room considered.

"I was thinking I should become a member," Bonnie said.

The librarian threw her head back and laughed, her right hand waiting above an open book.

Someone in the queue said: "I've never heard her laugh."

*

"Address?"

The librarian's hand hovered above the form. They were still in the library, Bonnie's books on a table. The children sat and watched Bonnie and their mother like hawks. Bonnie told her where she lived while she examined the neat part in the librarian's hair. Her hair was incredibly shiny. There was a scent of some sort. Musk.

"That's a bit out of our area."

"I told you last week where I lived."

"I'm teasing," the librarian said, still looking down. She wrote Bonnie's address in large block print.

"Phone number?"

"Why don't I fill it out."

She needed proof of residency.

"Bring it next time," the librarian said.

Bonnie gave the form back and the librarian stuck out a hand. "My name's Lee. It's a pleasure to meet you after all these weeks."

The daughter sidled closer to Bonnie during the handshake and smiled at Bonnie tentatively. The boy still sat at the table, his mouth as flat and thin as a line. Watching.

*

Something had clicked into place without warning, without sneakery, without tricks and swept Angela way back to some dark backwater. Bonnie was amazed. She had never approached love front on but had always waited for it to hit her first and hotwire her body. Her internal rules had somehow changed and she didn't need to worship from a distance and then be disappointed at hand's length.

She drove up and down beach roads thinking about this feeling, toying with its novelty. She parked the ute at Maroubra and watched the surf doing what it had done when she was a child, gently wash objects onto the sand and pound them to smithereens.

"Now what exactly is it?" she asked herself like a pep-talking coach, like an analyst. She was suspicious of her own motives and so flung herself on the couch. All she discovered was that she was proud of how she had accomplished this trauma-free, crush-free love. A single piece of driftwood skirted up on to the sand and stayed there.

Bonnie drove to the library.

"Hi, gorgeous!" Lee leaned across the counter and kissed her in front of two dozing men and a borrower. Bonnie stood blushing and shuffling.

"Are we having dinner tonight?"

Lee looked surprised. "Don't we have dinner together every night?"

"Just checking."

Lee was solid. There were no tricks. There was no disappearing for days on end. There was no husband. Bonnie still couldn't quite trust that Lee would be there when she turned up at the library but there she was, every time, stamping books, putting them back on the shelves. Lee's calm was a magnet for stray iron filings of emotion. Her face inside the storm of hair was open, waiting for whatever came along and accepting it before it happened. Lee had said: "I'm a librarian. I have two children. I've got brown hair. I'm not exactly a bargain. I'm more like pre-loved goods."

But sex with these pre-loved goods was extraordinary, shuttling the full length of some train of passion; slow, then fast, rollicking from one side of the bed to the other. Transporting them both and dumping them off with salt-slicked, juiced-up skin.

Bonnie couldn't imagine that Lee had a past, except that the evidence of her past deeds sat there every day, tugging on her hands, taking dinner plates from her, waiting at the library for her to take them home. The kids kept a safe distance from Bonnie, and she from them.

"Hey, tomorrow's Saturday," Lee whispered to Bonnie as she passed her table in the library. Bonnie was still in the Northern Territory. The down side of love, a very minor handicap, was the slackening of her research. Now when she imagined the towns, she saw Lee sitting in a cafe absorbed in a library book.

"We can sleep in," Bonnie said.

"Eat bacon and eggs."

"Drink coffee."

"Fuck."

Bonnie felt her groin curl up. Lee hovered around her table, all innocence. It seemed that she couldn't tear herself away. She whistled some hearty tune and bounced off. Readers lifted their heads from their books and looked at her with surprise. "Oops," she said. She disappeared behind the large print section and the whistle continued softly. Then stopped.

"Hey, honey! There's a good book here on birds of the West Australian coast."

Hello world! thought Bonnie, here we are!

Old men muttered and shifted.

Alice and William were transfixed by television. They took toast from their mother without looking up from the screen. Bonnie, not used to children, was attuned to their every move. She would question Lee about their diet, about whether they got enough exercise, about Will's suspicious lack of homework. She thought Lee was dangerously casual with them.

"Lee, should they be watching so much TV?"

"Probably not."

They were finishing breakfast, eating the saved corners of toast and egg.

"But it's just a music show Bon."

"Yeah, but have you noticed the stuff in videos these days? The naked women? The sexual connotations?"

Bonnie sounded like a quivering, offended aunt.

"Yes. Yes." Lee was so calm, with her thoughtful nodding of the head. She considered everything. "But some are quite good too. Where do I stop? And connections are only made if there's prior knowledge. If I jump up and down about them seeing a naked woman on a white horse they'll think, what's wrong with white horses? They'll think, what's wrong with naked women?"

"Yeah. I suppose." Bonnie was tired of the subject. "I don't know anything about kids."

"God, who does?"

Bonnie raised her head suddenly as if she could smell fire in the house.

"What's up?"

Bonnie turned her head towards the lounge room. That song. Her ears homed to it like arrows. It was a tune she could whistle in her sleep. Firetown, who she had secretly decided would founder without her in the drummer's seat, were playing 'Mantelpiece' on television.

"Will? Can you see the band playing?"

"Yeah."

"Can you see the drummer?"

Lee didn't know what was happening. Bonnie had not mentioned her drumming to her.

"What is it? What's going on?"

She wanted to know the lie of the land in her own house. Bonnie would have to tell her, now that she was acting so strangely.

"He's got a funny hat on," Alice reported.

Lee walked out to see for herself.

"Black hat?" Bonnie asked.

"Yeah," Lee said.

The drummer from Rust.

126

"Bastard!" Bonnie said under her breath. "Bastards."

"It looks like a fez."

Bonnie sat in a frieze of shock. She felt doublecrossed in a game she had abandoned long ago. She wanted to avenge a wrongful act. But who had committed it?

"He looks a bit pretentious," Lee said, "throwing his arms around like an idiot."

She came back into the dining room and sat down.

"So. Tell me the story."

Bonnie told her about Firetown. About drumming. About Angela. Lee sat astounded.

"How could you not tell me all that?"

Alice and Will came in to listen. Alice drowsed with a thumb in her mouth but her eyes were on Bonnie.

"Something that was so important in your life," said Lee.

"Not any more."

Bonnie couldn't have both things – a relationship and a band. Not two good things at once. When she did, both things turned bad. She wondered if she could ever put that in words so that Lee would understand. Lee stood behind Bonnie and hugged her.

"So, love of mine, is there anything else you want to tell me?"

"No. Anything you want to tell me?"

"I played second trombone in the Boston Symphony once."

"Very funny."

Alice had fallen asleep on the floor. She seemed to have a talent for falling asleep anywhere, usually wherever a conversation was taking place. Maybe the sound of voices soothed her. Lee bent down and traced some long hair out of her eyes. Alice sighed and turned over.

"And what about the Gale?"

"Ah, the Gale."

"When do you work on it? Why don't you ever talk about it?"

"I'm in it, aren't I Mum?" Will said. "But I've got red hair."

He threw words into the conversation like currants into cake. Just when Bonnie had forgotten he was in the room he would say something, but only to his mother, not her. His eyes followed Lee everywhere. His glances at Bonnie were carefully choreographed, as if he didn't want to notice her more than was absolutely necessary.

"I never talk about the Gale. I don't know why I did that day. No, yes, I do. I wanted you to know about me. I knew you were the type who thinks all lesbians have short hair."

"No I'm not," Bonnie said automatically.

Lee lifted the teapot to gauge its weight and went out into the kitchen.

Bonnie heard the grind and scrape of a match.

"I haven't worked on the Gale for a long time."

"Why not?"

Lee teetered on the edge of the subject and backed off.

"How did you know when you couldn't drum any more?"

"I didn't feel any rhythms. Normally I'm tapping something out on the table or in my teeth."

Lee came back in, a teaspoon in one hand, and stared at her.

"Your teeth?"

"I grind my teeth. Not loudly but it drives people crazy."

"I see. And this famous actress woman Angela dropped you and that was it. No more drums."

"I think so. Yes. Couldn't play without her around."

"Hmm."

They looked at each other.

"Pathetic, isn't it?" said Bonnie.

Lee came over and straddled her lap. Will sighed and went back to the TV. Lee ran her tongue inside the groove of Bonnie's lips.

"It's not pathetic," she whispered. "It's just not true. It can't be. Can we go upstairs now?"

The kettle screamed and Lee jumped up. Bonnie stayed at the table and stared at nothing. The television in the lounge room blared jungle music for a car advertisement. It sounded a bit like the *Naked City* feel at the Wastelandish Theatre, except faster. It'd sound good on Lee's boomy wooden kitchen table. The thought was a quick flicker. Alice sat up and rubbed at her face.

"My teeth feel all clickety!" she said.

"What do you mean?"

But Alice was looking right through Bonnie, as though she was talking to the window behind her. Bonnie realised that she was still asleep.

"All dried up," Alice said loudly and lay down again and closed her eyes.

*

Bonnie still thought about Angela. It was usually when she was doing automatic things — parking the ute, hanging out washing, cleaning her teeth. She would stop whatever she was doing and remember certain kisses or the view out of the Blackheath hotel room. Lee always seemed to sense it.

"Thinking about that Famous Actress Woman Angela?" she said the first time and looked in the mirror over Bonnie's shoulder. Bonnie tensed up, ready to deny it but Lee just smiled.

Bonnie had avoided watching *Sunday Live* but she came downstairs one

Sunday morning and found Lee sitting on the lounge, studying Angela's performance with her head slightly to one side. She looked up at Bonnie, said hello, and then looked back at the TV.

"I wish you wouldn't," Bonnie said finally.

"Sorry." Lee turned off the television. "I'm just a bit fascinated."

"Don't be."

"She was a big part of your life, Bon."

"Not really." Bonnie sat down and rubbed her eyes and yawned. Lee watched her.

"Why do you deny your past so much?"

Bonnie wondered sleepily whether she could deny that she denied her past without sounding ridiculous.

*

Bonnie set up a work space for Lee. She pushed her desk over to the window where the bed had been. Bought her an adjustable chair and a desk light. She found a quote from somewhere, typed it out and taped it to the wall for inspiration. She wiped down Lee's typewriter, stacked paper in crisp buildings on the right side of the desk.

Lee came in to inspect her newly arranged room. She spun around on the chair, noticed the paper taped to the wall and arched up to read it.

"'When I am working on a book or story I write every morning as soon after first light as possible.' Who said that?"

"Hemingway. It was the shortest quote I could find."

"It's perfect. Not crystally or new agey. I couldn't stand a quote about feminine energy above my head the whole day."

Bonnie stood up. "Well I'm off."

"Where are you going?"

"I'm taking Alice and William to the Botanic Gardens, remember? You even made the sandwiches."

"That's right. Oh well, have fun." Lee was already somewhere else in her head. Bonnie fought terror. This was her first excursion with children. She dawdled in the doorway, hoping Lee would say, what the heck I'll come too! But Lee had picked up a sheet of paper and was tapping it crisply against the desk.

*

Alice strapped herself into her seatbelt without any help, all tongue and thumbs, while Will and Bonnie waited. Bonnie listened for the tapping of Lee's typewriter to drift down from the window but there was only the sound of Alice's concentrated breathing. The car was hot. Will wound his window down, stuck his head out, pulled it back in and glared at Alice.

"Hurry up!"

"Shut up, Will Pill."

"Hey, you're swearing," Bonnie noticed.

"I can say shut up."

Bonnie put the car in first gear and it jumped forward.

"Shit," she muttered. She hadn't driven Lee's car before.

"Ha! You said shit!"

"What are we doing when we get there?"

Bonnie ground into second. "We're going to have lunch."

"My legs are stuck to the seat. Are there swings?"

"No."

"Can we go to a park with swings?"

"We're going to a grownup park," Will said.

They all pictured a grownup park. What was in it?

"What's in a grownup park?" asked Alice.

"Trees and specimens of plants," Will said as if reading from something. Boredom flattened his voice.

"Have you been there before, Will?"

He sighed with the tedium of it.

"Yeah. Dad and Mum and me went once."

Alice slapped Will's arm.

"Don't say Dad while she's here."

"Why not?" he roared. "Mum says Dad while she's around. Don't you hit me!"

There was the ugly sound of a thump, a short silence and then Alice's wail.

"He hit me!"

"Will. Don't hit her."

"Don't tell me what to do. You're not my mum!" Will said.

"You should hit him. Mum hits him if he hits me."

"There's too much hitting in the world," Bonnie said.

What should she do? Miraculously they settled again. Maybe this was a normal everyday sort of driving-along-in-the-car conversation. It was hard to tell what was normal and what wasn't. Bonnie felt sweat bead and trickle under her shirt as the car lurched along. By the time she parked in Art Gallery Road she was exhausted.

"My legs are still stuck to the seat," Alice said.

"Well, unstick them, stupid."

They sat under a fig tree in the Domain as a compromise because Alice spotted the swings and the Gardens seemed a long way away.

The basket was opened — chicken and salad sandwiches, cheese and ham sandwiches, a block of chocolate which Alice reached for. Bonnie hid it behind her and ended up sitting on it.

"Why didn't Mum come?" asked Alice.

"She's working on the Gale."

"Oh."

The Gale would become family myth whether it was written or not.

"I'm thirsty."

"I'll get some drinks from that ice cream van," Will offered.

Was that a good idea? Bonnie ran through possible disasters in her head: kidnap, car accident. She only had a ten dollar note. She handed it to him.

"Don't lose the change."

Her voice was so high and nervous with him. His mouth curled with scorn. She had an urge to throw more money at him as a bribe to get him to like her.

"Yeah, I know. I got pockets."

He took off and Alice watched him go, wide-eyed.

"What's wrong Alice?"

"Nothing. Hey, let's pretend we're on an island and this is our only food and there's no-one around. Look!" she pointed a finger at an old couple who were walking a dog. "Sharks! They want to eat us!"

"Oooh! They're getting closer," tried Bonnie. She ate a chicken sandwich. The garlic speckled mayonnaise that Lee made was fantastic.

"No! You have to be not speaking. Only I can talk. You're my prisoner let's make it," said Alice. She peeled the top half off a ham and cheese sandwich and threw the ham at the dog.

"If I feed the sharks they won't eat us."

"Alice."

"See? They're going away now."

The old couple had turned toward the round restaurant. The dog snuffled and devoured the ham and now circled the grass, its nose down. The man whistled him closer. The old couple were going to sit on that terrace and drink coffee. Maybe read the weekend papers in a comfortable silence. Bonnie pictured it. She was craving coffee, black and bitter.

Will appeared with his arms full of sweet booty – cans of Coke and creaming soda – and in one hand three ice creams that melted and dripped onto the food.

"Mum only lets us have minial water," said Alice. She tore the paper off her ice cream.

"Well, this is a treat then. Where's the change, Will?"

"There was none." Will said, his face blank but his mouth smeared with the signs of rapid feasting. If Bonnie pretended to believe him, would he like her? Or would he think she was stupid?

"Hey!" Alice said to her. "Can we —"

"Call me Bonnie."

"Can we swing now, Bonnie?"

"After lunch."

Alice and Will looked at each other. After they had eaten the ice creams and then lunch, the three of them walked over to the swings. Alice and Will sat down and curled their hands into fists around the rusty iron chains. They worked on propelling themselves up in long arcs, Will throwing his head backwards as he swung down to earth.

"Do you want me to push you?" Bonnie asked.

"Nuh."

"Alice?"

"No. Thanks."

Bonnie sat on the ground and watched them. After five minutes or so they got off the swings and walked over to the slide. They didn't look at Bonnie but somehow she understood she was to follow them over and keep watching. She found a seat under another fig tree and obediently kept her eyes on them. They didn't seem to talk to each other but from where she was she couldn't be sure. Maybe they had an intricate sort of code they used that no-one else could understand.

They played as though they were still in the library. They coasted quietly and efficiently down the slide, their expressions not changing, and then walked back to the ladder and climbed up again. Whenever it was Alice's turn to climb, Will had to go up as well. He then pushed her from the top rung to a sitting position at the very top. Once there, she sat and looked around the park, sometimes looking at Bonnie and then looking quickly away. Bonnie sensed that Will had instructed her that they weren't to communicate with her.

A clump of family walked over to the slide. The father had two kids by one hand. They were worshipping him as they walked, pulling at his hands so that he looked like a lumbering marionette. The mother walked separately, her arms quiet and still by her sides. She was overshadowed.

"Dad! Let's go on the slide! Dad!"

He hoisted the smaller girl onto his shoulders and piggybacked her over to where Will and Alice, seated on her throne at the top, were watching him. The overshadowed mother came and sat next to Bonnie on the seat.

"Hi."

"Hi."

"G'day kids!" he said. His voice travelled clear across the park. Will said something inaudible and gave him a big smile. Little bugger, thought Bonnie. You've never smiled at me like that.

The man sat the girl in front of Alice.

"Down you go!" He gave her a shove. Alice and Will watched her hit the dirt screeching with laughter and get scooped up again by her father. The other kid was tugging at his arm.

"Dad, Dad."

"Hang on a tick," Dad boomed. "Let this little girl go first. Down you go honey!" The three of them waited politely for Alice.

Alice had no choice. She came down the slide like an ageing princess, her bare legs skidding and shrieking on the metal. Will slid down and came to a halt behind her. Without a word to each other, they walked over to Bonnie and stood in silence.

"Had enough, hey?" the overshadowed mother said. "Getting Mum to take you home?" She raised her eyebrows and parted her lips in a big smile in a desperate attempt at cheeriness.

"She's not our mother," Will said icily.

"Oh ..."

Bonnie watched her face cave back into its disappointed shape. Both women sat and swung their feet like children.

"She's not from our place," Alice explained, "she's a lesbian."

On the way home Bonnie sat alone in the front like a chauffeur. The children sat together in the back, grim and silent as stone statues. When they were nearly home Will sought out her eyes in the rearview mirror.

"My Dad plays the guitar," he said.

"Does he?"

For some reason she felt jealous.

"And he plays the harmonica."

Bonnie clenched the steering wheel until her knuckles were white.

"Does he really?"

"Yeah. Can you?"

"No." She coughed a dry little inactive cough.

"I can play the monica," Alice said.

"No you can't," Will said. "You just hold it up to your mouth and pretend. Dad really goes for it. I really like my Dad."

The car lurched forward.

"He's a good driver too."

*

"He really said that? The little so and so."

Lee on the bed and stroked Bonnie's hair. Bonnie was clamped onto Lee as though she might fly off the bed and out the window.

"Do you ever say the word lesbian to them? Do they know what it means?"

"Will flinches when I say it so, yes, he knows. Alice thinks it's like a nationality or something. Her best friend's Spanish, her mother's lesbian, that type of thing."

"I gathered that."

"Yeah well ..."

They rarely talked about the kids. Lee seemed to skirt the subject as if sensing trouble. But now in the dark she suddenly said, "It's Will whose the problem."

"Why?"

Lee shrugged. A tiny sound.

"I bet I know why. He wants his Dad. It's obvious. All boys want their Dad around."

"Mmm."

"Where is their Dad?"

"Tasmania. He loafs around on a half acre block and fishes."

"I loaf around."

"You don't loaf. You're artistic. You play drums."

"So why doesn't Will go and see him?"

"He is going to see him."

"Oh."

"Next week. He's going down for two weeks. Alice is going too."

Bonnie tried not to feel her heart lighten.

"Why didn't you tell me?"

Lee sighed.

"I don't know. I never like talking about him."

There was a silence.

"So can he play the harmonica?"

"Badly. He also renovates furniture badly, runs a hardware shop badly and looks after his kids badly. He's a pretty good drinker, though."

"G'night honey."

"G'night."

Bonnie pulled the sheet right up to her chin and watched street light tinker with the colour of the walls. It flickered in white bars across the book shelves. Lee had books lined along every wall of the house, except the bathroom. She was addicted to the printed word. But her books at home were not catalogued by the Dewey decimal system. They were a random assembly. She kept her overflow of fiction in the kids' rooms, so that Alice's Little Golden Books were wedged alongside *All That False Instruction* and *Lives of Girls and Women*. She had dictionaries scattered through the house so that she could look up words easily. She even had a special shelf for books she hadn't read yet. Bonnie smiled at the ceiling. Bonnie didn't loaf, Lee had asserted, she drummed. Lee's faith in her was astounding but it would run out.

9

Melanie's hands cupped the spinning brown lump. Mud washed over her fingers in rivulets. Nora and Bonnie sat with their feet up on a wooden box and watched her work. A cylinder formed, Melanie dug in her thumbs and the cylinder had a lip.

"It's amazing that someone who works in a library would want to write novels. You'd think she'd have decided that there were enough of them around."

Bonnie scowled at Nora.

"It's amazing that an English teacher who can recite T S Eliot would want to sing 'I'm a Little Teapot' at kids parties."

"What about your drumming?"

"Yeah," Melanie said, as if Nora had stated an opinion. Clay dotted her hair where she had brushed it back with her fingers. "Not many women drummers around. We need more of them."

Bonnie looked around the garden. The tropical fruits were still in a messy clump against the fence after all this time: tiny clay mangoes, pineapples and watermelons exactly where they were on the day Bonnie first saw them. Nothing had any effect except weather and age. Nora still wore her Jessie beanie, perched at a strange angle over one eye. Underneath it, her hair was streaked with grey. Bonnie saw it for the first time and it gave her a strange ache. She looked away, suddenly angry.

"Look at us sitting around! We never earn any money. We're all poor. I play drums, Nora's a clown at kid's parties, you make all these pots but you can't afford to get your lawn mowed. I don't own a car. We're all dreaming!"

Melanie looked up, the smile dropped from her face.

"Become a merchant banker then. Anyway I thought you'd stopped playing."

"And the lawn does get mowed," Nora said. "I just do a bad job. And didn't Belle lend you her car?"

They weren't taking her seriously. Bonnie went for the bone.

"And how have you two managed to stay together so long anyway?"

Nora took her feet off the box so that it toppled over and Bonnie's legs fell onto the grass.

"We stuck at it. We work out our problems. Maybe you should try it! Stick at something instead of chucking it in. I'm making tea."

She stomped off across the lawn.

Bonnie shouted out, "You were the one who dumped me, remember? You chucked it in with me. I want *coffee.*"

Nora stopped. They both looked at Melanie as if waiting for her to sort them out but Melanie had her face down at pot level. Her nose practically touched it. Nora disappeared into the house. Bonnie coughed, embarrassed.

"Anne's stopped me working on her lists," she said. She knew Melanie was trying to concentrate but perversely she talked on.

"She didn't get any backing from the car rental places. She's going to try other ways but it doesn't look good."

"Have you gone on the dole?"

"I was always on it. Anne only paid me in bits at a time. Never enough to live on."

"What are you going to do?"

"Moan about it for a bit."

"And when you've done that?"

"Don't know."

"Something will come up."

"That's very passive thinking," Bonnie said.

"Yes, it is."

Bonnie, swilling around in her bad mood, couldn't tell if Melanie was being sarcastic or if she agreed with Bonnie. It infuriated her. She felt this anger with a dull surprise. She had a drought of tenderness in her, she decided. There would only ever be this simmer of anger, accompanied by the despairing scraping trundle of Melanie's wheel. Except now she had Lee. Bonnie thought of Lee, sitting at home with her nose in a book, and something melted in the pit of her stomach.

"I've moved in with Lee."

"Good."

"Why's it good?"

"Bonnie what's wrong with you today? She's a good person, that's why." Melanie sat back and looked at the raw pot on the wheel. Every fibre of her was pointed at it, examining it for flaws maybe, or just shooting out rays of admiration and happiness. Bonnie thought it looked like all the other pots that sat around on dusty ledges and in corners of the studio. Nora was back with a tray. She put it down carefully and looked at the freshly thrown pot.

"That's a fantastic one."

Obviously there was something Bonnie wasn't seeing. She felt that they were leaving her out of some big secret. Maybe in order to feel creative again she would have to put in a bit more effort.

"It sure is," she said. Nora and Melanie looked at her, as though checking that she really meant it.

*

136

That night Lee showed her the beginning of the Gale.

"Just so you know it does exist."

Showing Bonnie her work brought out some coy, nervy side in Lee. She paced the floor and glanced at the bit of manuscript that Bonnie was holding. She squeezed her hair into a nervous pony tail.

"It has to be reworked of course."

"OK."

"I need lots of potential conflict to get it up and running."

"Lee, I can't concentrate if you talk to me."

"Sorry. I'll go and make dinner."

But she continued to hover while Bonnie read. There wasn't much action in the Gale yet. Lengthy weather descriptions set a mood of foreboding. Two women were secretly in love, one had a son and daughter (surprise surprise) and was unhappily married. The characters snorted, exclaimed, gasped and murmured. A sex scene on the fourth page made Bonnie stare at Lee.

"Where did you get the idea for this?"

Lee pulled her hair out of its pony tail and then stuffed it back again. She picked up a hairbrush and put it down with a clatter.

"When I was married I had a whole stockpile of fantasies. That's one of them." She yanked at her hair again. "Well, a couple of them."

"Sheesh." Three women in a boat with a bottle of coconut oil.

"Is it too much?"

"It gets you in."

"So do you like it?"

Bonnie pictured Melanie's little pot sitting on the potter's wheel.

"I think it's great."

"Do you?"

"I'd expand on it. You could even have the boat in the water."

"You reckon?"

"I reckon."

Lee drew in her breath. She circled Bonnie with her arms and kissed her.

They waltzed around the tiny room and then fell onto the bed. They made love slowly, Lee buoyed and bursting and leading the way. Bonnie slow and sluggish, worrying about her life right up to the second before she came with her mouth against Lee's throat. The sound of the television came up through the floor to where they lay on the bed. The kids would be sitting downstairs on the carpet in open-mouthed attendance. Lee murmured something.

"What?" Bonnie asked.

"The boat. It could be *rocking* in the water as a symbol of passion."

*

Will's room was small. It was like a monk's cell that smelt not of candle wax or ancient parchment but of boy. Lee often went through it to look for things he wouldn't show her. She would remove objects she didn't approve of, such as a water pistol and an aluminium baseball bat. Strangely, he wasn't outraged. He accepted that his mother had a perfect right to order his life. But Bonnie was still shocked to find Lee looking under his mattress the night after he'd gone to Tasmania.

"People who snoop are always sorry."

"Is that an ancient proverb? Or some modern Bonnie wisdom?" Lee pulled out two pages. "Here it is."

"Jesus Christ, Lee!"

"Relax. I just want you to read something. There's something we should sort out."

"I really don't want to." But Bonnie was reading it even as she protested. 'Dear Will. Im soory for the figt,' the note said.

Glitter was sprinkled heavy-handedly around the writing.

"Will and Alice had a fight last week."

"What about?"

"What about? Um, about you."

"Where was I?"

"You were at Nora and Melanie's."

This family was so self-contained. They had secrets from her, codes that were set in time. They were related by blood. Certain things, she saw for the first time, would never change.

"So what was the fight about?"

"Will wrote this composition."

Lee looked down at the other page she was holding and then half held it out. Bonnie grabbed it.

> My family
> I live with Mum and Dad and Alice. Alice is my sister. Mum
> is tall, so is dad. Mum works in a libry where men sleep. Dad and
> I fished in a river and I caught a brim. Dad says never to fish under
> a brige but upstream. Dad fixes the roof when it leaks.

Will's neat print across the page had rendered her invisible in eight words. And the roof-fixing detail was downright evil. The paper shook in her hand. She wanted to screw it up and burn it. She wanted to say something horrible.

"Caught a brim? What was he fishing for? Hats?"

"Yeah, his spelling leaves a lot to —"

"And why did he stuff it under his mattress?"

"He was upset so he hid it. Alice told him he was a liar. They hardly ever fight with each other. They're a little team usually."

Bonnie remembered Alice and Will sitting in the library for hours. And then fighting in the car. About what? About mentioning their father in front of her. She saw them suddenly as frightened and vulnerable.

"They know how important you are to me," Lee said.

"Well that's the problem. I'm the most important person to come into this house since their father."

Lee opened her mouth to say something and then closed it.

"It's an occasion if a friend of yours visits, let alone if some stranger moves in!"

"Well —"

"Let alone someone sleeping in their mother's bed." Bonnie wondered how she came to be defending Will's actions.

"I suppose so."

"Let alone with their mother."

"OK, OK!"

"When I first saw your house I thought, God, Lee's buried herself in books. You're so self sufficient. You don't need anything else in your life."

"What's this got to do with the kids?"

"They're not used to you *needing* anyone. You hardly need them. You're not affectionate with them. Then they see us kissing and it's no wonder they're pissed off. So Will tries to write me out of his life. He's pretending you're still happily married."

"So you think I've neglected them?" Lee considered calmly. "Maybe I should write to them."

"Why don't you just ring them?"

But Lee was already sitting at Will's tiny desk clearing a space with her forearm.

"Their father can't afford a phone."

She ripped a page of lined paper out of an exercise pad and flattened it out on the desk. Then she picked up a pen and tapped it twice on the wood surface. "Hmm."

"Are you sure you want to do this? I mean, you don't have to do it just because I said so."

It was a novelty to see her thoughts result in action. No-one had respected them that much. Except maybe when she was drumming.

"You're right though. There's stuff that I should do —"

Lee started writing on the paper. The house was incredibly quiet without the constant chat of television. Pinned to the wall above the desk was a 'Fishes of the Australian Coast' poster. Bonnie imagined Will writing his little composition and glancing up at the wall. He might have been inspired by the bream and added it in. It was all a bit sad. Bream wasn't even a river fish. And here was his mother sitting in the same tiny chair, writing her own composition of hope and proffered love.

"How's this?" Lee sat up straight and held the page out in front of her. "Hi kids, what are you up to? Bonnie and I are fine. The library is as busy as ever. Mrs O'Hara came in and said where are my children? meaning you two of course! We miss you already even though you only left yesterday. Bonnie is … " she looked at Bonnie, "that's as far as I've got."

"Bonnie is … Bonnie is what? Tired? Cooking at the moment? Horny?" Lee grinned sheepishly.

"I don't know. I just wrote it."

Bonnie lay on her back on Will's bed and threw her feet up against the wall. She could see the scuff marks where Will had done the same thing with his shoes.

"Write: Bonnie is going to cook you a big welcome home meal."

"Are you?"

"Yeah, why not."

Four days later the phone rang. Bonnie got out of the shower to answer it and heard beeps.

"Hello?"

There was a sudden rush of coins.

"You hold the rest."

"Hello?"

"Hello Bonnie?"

"Alice is that you?"

"Yeah."

"Where are you?"

"In a phone box."

She heard Will's voice in the background. "Phone *booth.*"

"We want to come home."

"What's wrong?"

"We don't like Dad any more." Her voice suddenly went quavery.

"Alice, put Will on for a second."

"Is Mummy home?"

"No honey she's —"

"Hello Bonnie."

"Will! What's happening?"

"Dad's getting drunk all the time. He says stuff about Mum and Alice starts crying."

She looked at the circle of drops on the carpet around her and shivered slightly.

"Do you want us to come and get you?"

"Come and *get* us?"

"Yeah, fly down there and get you."

"Um."

Bonnie was certain it was what they should do. She imagined the scene at the airport as Will and Alice, waiting in a corner, jumped up when Bonnie strode in. They would fall into Bonnie's arms gratefully – Bonnie the lesbian who never drank and who played her instrument well. Used to play her instrument well.

"Does that mean we won't get the dinner?" Will asked.

"What dinner?'

"Our big welcome home dinner."

"You'll still get that. We'll fly down tonight. OK?"

"Wow ... all right."

"Does your mother know the address down there?"

"Yeah."

There was a huge roar and then the squeal of brakes.

"What was that?"

"Just a truck."

She tried to not to imagine Alice lying unconscious on a highway.

"OK. Well, we'll see you at eight o'clock then."

Eight o'clock? Where did she get that from? But Will didn't seem to care that she had just plucked a time out of the air. It was her job to do that. She was the adult. He had confidence in her. She booked two flights to Hobart and then rang Lee at the library.

"You did the right thing." Lee said.

"Yeah I know."

"Thanks Bon."

"My pleasure."

*

Lee's hand was a fist in Bonnie's lap. She stared out of the aeroplane window even though the view was just blackness and a blinking red wing light. Bonnie decided to distract her.

"Dyke."

"What?"

"Definite dyke. That air hostess over there."

Lee didn't even turn her head. She swivelled her eyes around. "Hmm. Could be."

"No question. Look, she just smiled at me!"

"Uhuh."

Bonnie sighed. "I'm going to read for a bit."

She pulled *A Fringe of Leaves* from her bag. On Lee's recommendation she was giving it another try. The pages felt crisp and dry in the air of the cabin.

"Once Will came back with scabies," Lee said.

"Hey?"

"When he came back from Hobart once. I shouldn't have let the kids go down. He's got a girlfriend who's in some religious sect apparently. And Alice and Will always come back with colds." Lee was speaking quickly but in a high dreamlike voice as if she had detached herself somehow. "Sorry about all this drama."

But Bonnie was enjoying this mercy dash. She felt useful. It was Lee who hated the drama. She was acting very unLeelike. She was fidgeting. She took everything out of her seat pocket, smoothed it out and then thrust it back in.

"I've decided that I like to know where people are," she said. She straightened the edge of the air sickness bag. Bonnie pictured her cataloguing everyone and laughed. But Lee didn't smile.

"I'm worried about the kids, Bonnie."

"I know." Suddenly nothing was funny.

At Hobart they walked out of the airport without needing to wait for luggage. It was a frosty night. A single cab waited at the taxi rank and after Lee had given an address to the driver they huddled together in the back. Town lights gave way very quickly to darker streets, lit only occasionally by single yellow lamps. Bonnie felt excited about being in a foreign place. About flying over the water to somewhere new. She wanted to nudge Lee and point at the beret the driver was wearing. She wanted to say: 'What's that? Local costume?' But she wanted to be an adult even more, so she said, "How should we handle this?"

"I'll go in and get them. You stay in the taxi."

"I don't want to stay in the taxi. I always have to stay in the car." She heard her petulant tone.

Lee frowned. "What do you mean?"

"Nothing."

"When have I ever —"

"Not you. Other people."

"Well, you go and get the kids then."

"What's the father's name? I don't even know his name."

Lee stared at her as if she had remembered something and then leaned forward and said, "Just here thanks."

The taxi stopped and Bonnie opened her door.

"I'll stay in the car," Lee said.

The road was half gravel, half tar. Bonnie found herself at the edge of what looked like a playground that sloped up towards a small weatherboard house. A tyre swing hovered next to a small plastic slippery dip. Its base was loaded with sacks. A dog barked somewhere. She started to walk up towards the house. Her feet slid on long wet grass. Halfway up the slope she tripped over something. She swore to herself and then peered down at whatever it was, her mouth chugging nervous vapour out into the air. Square, red, green. Alice's little rucksack. She stopped breathing and listened. The taxi motor gurgled down behind her. She moved her head to one side slowly. She sensed someone near her.

"Alice?" she called softly.

There was a furtive skidding noise from the slippery dip. Then the sacks detached themselves and moved towards her.

Then Alice was whispering "Bonnie". Will was on her other side, holding his rucksack. Both children were trying to share the one blanket. Now that they had moved from their spot, one corner hung in the wet grass. Will took her hand. "Let's go." He spoke very flatly. He seemed smaller than usual, shrivelled by something.

"Do you want me to talk to your Dad?" She could feel his dry little palm. She had never felt his skin before.

"No."

"Did you have anything else we need to get?"

Something in her wanted to extend the rescue. She wanted to meet him, the nameless husband-father. But the children were pulling her back down the slope. Lee, who had started climbing, knelt down and hugged Alice. There was a shout from somewhere. "Lee? Lee!"

Lee straightened up almost guiltily.

"It's Dad!" hissed Alice.

Up at the house a figure stood looking down from the verandah.

"Get up here. I wanna talk to you!"

The taxi driver was standing on the road next to his cab, slowly realising that some sort of family drama was unfolding. He scratched his head through the beret.

"Is that bloke up there coming as well?" he asked Bonnie.

"No he's not." Bonnie opened the back door and pushed Alice and Will into the car. She got in next to Alice and put her arms around her. She could feel that Alice was only just holding on. Her body was shaking with the effort.

The taxi driver said, "Well, I'm glad about that," and spat carefully on the road. "He looks like a big bastard from here." .

"Who's that woman? Your girl friend?" the voice called out. "Is that Bonnie?"

"He read Mum's letter. That's when he started," Will said.

"Where's Mum?" Alice said. They looked around for her. The taxi driver said, "I thought she was with you."

The voice from the house gave a pained sort of laugh. "Hey Lee come here. I wanna show you something."

"She's up there!" Bonnie bolted out of the cab, sprinted up the hill and stopped when she saw Lee gazing up at the house, smearing her hands up and down her hips, like a child facing something awful.

"Lee, let's go."

"I need to say something to him," Lee said to Bonnie in her high floating detached voice "but I don't know what. He still terrifies the shit out of me. Can you believe that?"

And then she gave a deranged rasp of a giggle. The man on the verandah was tugging at his pants.

"Remember this?"

He toppled sideways slightly and swore under his breath as though a carefully choreographed piece was now ruined. He steadied himself on the front railing and staggered however many steps it took to make his way down to where Lee and Bonnie stood.

"Christ, no," Bonnie said.

The light was milky on the lawn between him and them and as he got closer his shadow loomed large. Bonnie wanted to walk down the hill but stood, as if she'd been sucked into Lee's wary, shaking vacuum. If I knew his name, she thought, it wouldn't be so bad. If he was a Donald or a Bill I could scream it out. He was closer and then he was standing, swaying, in a T shirt and his mouth was working up to saying something. He had greying stubble, Bonnie saw in a blink of detail, and scared, angry eyes. She floated up and stood right in front of him. She became some blurred foreign shadow who could say quite calmly, "Don't you fucking touch her! Don't you ever touch her!"

Bonnie took Lee's hand and led her down the hill.

"Fuckin' ... bitch," his voice behind them said.

The wet grass squeaking beneath their boots.

"When you asked me what his name was I couldn't remember. I tried to picture his face and I couldn't see it," Lee said.

"It doesn't matter." Bonnie led her to the cab.

"I can't believe you did that. It was fantastic."

She couldn't believe it either.

"Get in the back, honey."

Lee sat and cradled Alice absently. Will sat bolt upright next to them. He was staring at Bonnie, who sat with the driver.

"Let's go."

"Sure thing." He dragged on an inch of cigarette and flicked the butt out of the window.

"Back to the airport, thanks."

She felt as though she were leading them to safety. She wished that she could be driving them, rather than the bereted driver who was singing 'Private Dancer' to himself now that they were safely away. She looked at her reflection in the window, superimposed onto the passing houses.

"No more flights tonight, love."

"What?"

"No flights going anywhere this late, but I can take you to a nice hotel."

"Well …"

She turned around to ask Lee about money but she was asleep, with Alice tucked under her chin. Will still sat unblinkingly awake. Shock kept his body rigid and guarded. Poor kid, Bonnie thought, and remembered his little raspy hand.

"What do you think, Will? Will?"

He opened his mouth with effort.

"Let's go to a hotel," he said slowly.

She winked at him and he smiled right at her.

*

Now when Lee sat hunched over the Gale, Bonnie took the children out to parks, films and fairgrounds. She sat with mothers on grass verges and benches while Will and Alice played on swings, slides and dodgems. She listened to other people's stories about their kids and would nod sagely at shared foibles and familiar episodes. She waited until she had their attention and then she would tell a story of her own and then say: "Well, Will and Alice aren't actually mine, they're my girlfriend's children. But you can tell that once you look at their eyes. Their mother has the most gorgeous blue eyes as well."

Her body felt loose and jumpy. She had a feeling that she was waiting for something. Waiting contentedly with her hands idle and swinging.

Alice had taken a fancy to a row of suspended metal rings in one playground and she swung herself from one to the other, shouting, 'Bonnie, look, watch'. Her arms looked as though they would be pulled out of their sockets. Bonnie watched and then, after Alice had swung along the row and back again three times, had to blow on the white, hot blisters on her hands to cool them while Alice stood, grass-stained, panting and hot.

She entered their world of difficulties. She had forgotten about the problems that besiege children in primary school. Now when they came home from school they went to Bonnie with their homework. Lee came home later and said, "I miss them not being in the library."

"Will's got an assignment," Bonnie would say.

When that happened Lee would walk over to kiss her and whisper "I adore you," as though Bonnie had spoken extraordinary words of love.

Bonnie sat with Will in his room and tried to explain maths to him while he tapped and fidgeted. His pen cracked between his teeth.

"Why do I have to times both sides?"

"I don't know. It's a formula."

Maths was a given, she wanted to tell him. You just do it, like you live life. But his spelling! That was something that she had control over. She tested him.

"Guitar."

"Gee eye tea aye are."

"No."

She spelt it out and made him spell it back to her.

"Saxophone."

He looked sorrowfully at her. "Too hard."

"Don't give me that cute look. How do you know till you've tried?"

It was something her mother used to say to her. She heard it and smiled to herself. "All right then. Family."

"I know that."

He spelt it.

"And I can spell library. Mum taught me."

"All right smartie, can you spell my name?"

He grinned. "Too hard."

Alice's room was forested with dolls, bears, plastic monsters, pink clothes and half-finished drawings. A half-collapsed mosquito net hung over her bed. It had been hanging like that since Bonnie could remember and Alice slept on its mesh quite happily every night, waking up in the morning with most of it wrapped around her. Bonnie came in and sat on Alice's tiny chair.

"Play the bear game!" Alice said.

Bonnie leaned over and picked up a teddy bear from the floor.

"What's this one's name?" she asked.

"Her name's Alice."

"And this one?"

"Alice."

"And this one?"

"Her name's Alice too." She came to sit on Bonnie's lap. "But I might change her name, you know."

"Really?"

"I might change it to something starting with B!"

"What starts with B?"

"Bonnie!"

146

"Oh!"

That was the teddy bear game.

Careful paintings that had taken hours to finish were pinned by their dog-eared corners onto a wall or left under the bed. There was usually a princess with blonde Doris Day hair. Sometimes she rode a pony, sometimes she just stood stoutly on the page. She always held a pink handbag the size of a door.

"My kids adore you now," Lee said one night. "Will asks where you are every five minutes if you're out. Alice chats about you to her friends."

Bonnie felt a thrill. "What does she say?"

"She says you're a better cook than me."

"Anything else?"

"Well, she had a long conversation about meat and how you cook it and I don't."

Bonnie felt deflated. She had imagined an entirely different conversation: 'I've got a new lesbian mother', Alice would tell her friends as they opened their lunch boxes. 'Really?' her friends would ask chattily. 'What does she do?'

'She's a ...' but the matter of career was not settled yet and the scene faded from Bonnie's head. She imagined what school would be like by the time Alice was in Year 12. Education would be different. There'd be lesbian this and lesbian that. Older girls would hold hands in the playground.

One night in the kitchen Bonnie felt a tug on her sleeve as she stood breaking fists of pasta into rolling water. She looked down. Will and Alice stood like a deputation, solemn and full of a request. She reached down and peeled hair out of Alice's eyes.

"Bonnie can you take us to see *The Horse That Flew?*"

"Which horse that flew?"

"A new movie. It's a cartoon. Please?"

"I suppose."

"On Saturday while Mum's working on the Gale?"

"Yeah, OK."

But in the end they all went to see it. They stopped to examine the poster in George Street.

"Some American thing is it? Like *Bambi?*" asked Lee, peering at the lurid technicolour with suspicion. They stood in the queue with other mothers, fathers and children. Will roamed around and stared at people, too restless to stand still. Bonnie sent him off to buy Minties. Alice wore her full pink flotilla and held a white bear like an accessory. *The Horse That Flew* turned out to be an Australian film.

"Fantastic!" Lee said.

"Mum, who cares?" said Will and she cuffed him. They settled in the fourth row — Lee, then Bonnie, then Alice and then Will in the aisle seat. Will loaded Minties into his pocket and put three in his mouth before Lee reached over and grabbed the bag. Alice pushed a finger into Bonnie's arm.

"If I fall asleep you have to wake me up."

"All right."

The horse was a baby seahorse who had lost its mother and father when it had gone to play with its friend the starfish. The seahorse was scared the parents had been caught in a driftnet.

"I don't think that could happen," whispered Lee. "Wouldn't seahorses just go through a driftnet?"

The pink seahorse bobbed up and down the coast and asked different animals if they had seen its parents. The sea teemed with marine life. Shoals of beautiful tropical fish danced in every corner. There were technicolour explosions of coral but no-one could enjoy them because the seahorse was such a clumsy swimmer its survival was the only thing that mattered. It was out in the depths long before it should be. It bumped into things and it nearly swallowed a fish hook. Its little wings fluttered frantically. Its tail curled in a pathetic upside down question mark.

Bonnie eyes started to prickle. Her nose hurt. She squeezed Lee's hand.

"What's wrong?"

Bonnie shook her head and snuffled, concentrating on not sobbing aloud. Alice and Will, dry-eyed, watched her with interest. God, what the hell was wrong? Her body had become a flood and dried up crusts were breaking up, loosening and floating up to the surface.

"Why are you crying?" Alice asked. She gave Bonnie her bear.

"Something in my eye," Bonnie said. She blotted her eyes with the Alice bear."

Lee hooked her arm up with her own and patted her hand.

"Have a mintie." Will flicked one at her lap but it fell short and landed on the floor. "Oops." He bent over to look for it and banged his head on the seat in front of him.

"Oh, for crying out loud!" an adult voice said.

The seahorse had made an enemy – an evil grey nurse shark with jaws that glinted like Gargantuan versions of the perfect teeth in a toothpaste ad. The shark shadowed the seahorse.

"Come with me," it said "I will look after you."

"I saw a shark once," Will said loudly. "It was bigger than that."

Everyone knew it was a bad shark by its cunning voice. Characters in these colour cartoons were always so black and white, Bonnie thought. Her tears dried as she tried to place the shark voice. Will and Alice sat motionless in their seats. The little seahorse hovered. The shark circled more tightly. A decision was imminent. Everyone leaned forward in their seats. Little seahorse moved closer to the mouth of the cave. The rocks around its entrance were jagged as teeth. Bones of the shark's victims were arranged in piles but it was as though seahorse was blind because now it moved merrily towards them, its question mark tail curling and uncurling.

"At last. A bit of action," Will said.

"No!" Children screamed as though it was pantomime. "Don't go in there!"

The shark voice still niggled at Bonnie.

Alice stood up in her seat. "Hey! You stupid seahorse!"

"Oh, for crying out loud," from the seat in front.

Bonnie pulled her down.

"Go in!" Will called out. People turned and shushed him angrily.

"Gee kids," said Lee. "Remind me to take you to the pictures more often."

"You'll find everything to your satisfaction I'm sure," purred the grey nurse. What a strangely formal shark it was. Bonnie's mouth opened.

"It can't be!"

People turned and looked at her.

Bonnie pushed her mouth against Lee's ear.

"That's Angela Corbina."

"Where?"

"She's the shark. That's her *voice.*"

"What? The Famous Actress Woman Angela? You sure?"

Lee put her arm around her. Bonnie put her cheek against Lee's sleeve, which had the comforting smell of washing powder.

"Are you all right? Do you want to leave?"

"No. I want to see how it ends."

Why was Angela doing something like this? Wasn't it beneath her? Had her career suffered? Was she reduced to doing this sort of stuff because of her relationship with Bonnie?

The little seahorse hovered at the cave mouth fretting with indecision. Its body seemed to pulse in different colours, changing hues like a chameleon. Suddenly it turned around and fluttered up towards the surface. The shark gave a doglike snarl of disappointment, as if somehow it could not chase the seahorse any longer. Bonnie imagined Angela standing at a microphone, making that noise because she thought it could adequately represent the anger of a slighted shark in a children's cartoon. Now the camera was somehow angling straight down into the water so that as the seahorse ascended it grew bigger and bigger. The water turned from the bruised blue of deep dangerous water to a cheery light turquoise. A sigh of relief surfed up and down the rows of audience.

"See?" said Will through a new lump of mintie. "I knew it wouldn't go in."

"I knew it wouldn't too," Alice said.

The shark was now a circling black dot below the surface. Bonnie let out a long breath she'd been holding for ages.

10

They stood blinking outside in George Street. Jazz music came floating down to the footpath from somewhere.

"Let me just say to all of you what an interesting experience that was," Lee said.

"There's a man smiling at you, Bonnie," said Alice. Bonnie followed Alice's finger and saw someone wearing jeans with a hole in one knee. Gaffer tape was plastered on the spot in a cross shape. Glasses glinted. Wiry black hair exploded.

Jacob.

He walked over.

"I was just at the bus stop when I thought to myself, I know that haircut a mile away. Those unkempt locks."

She laughed, shook her head and smeared her eyes with a hand. Her other hand was still locked into Lee's.

"This is Lee. Lee, this is Jacob. And this is Alice and Will."

"Hello."

Will stood back and examined Jacob as though he was a rare specimen. Jacob stood and beamed, impervious.

"You're looking healthy Bonnie."

"I've stopped smoking."

"I've tried to ring you."

"I've moved out of Darlinghurst."

He nodded and flashed a quick smile at Lee.

"So are you drumming?"

She shook her head no. "What about you?"

Jacob smiled with some small remembered pleasure. "Yeah, I've taken up guitar again."

He had the same sleepy late-night look he'd had a year and a half ago. Tired but eternally optimistic. She imagined that if she leaned forward closer to him that he would smell of old, wrenched-up gaffer tape, of spilled beer and carpet.

"Listen," she said. "Give me a ring sometime."

"I don't have your number."

Lee offered Bonnie her ticket stub. Bonnie wrote her number on it and then Jacob ran for his bus, waving goodbye with a windmilling arm. Lee and Bonnie and the children drifted up the street.

The music was coming from a trio that had wedged themselves into an office doorway somehow. The drummer had found room for his snare drum and a ride cymbal in front of the step where he was sitting. The bass player sat on his amp. They were young, probably Conservatorium students, judging by their gravity. Their eyes never left their charts. People stopped to watch the drummer, whose eyes watched the crowd without seeing it. He had them mesmerised. His arms barely moved but his hands bounced and flicked the sticks up and back. Accents popped. Bonnie pulled Lee right next to her.

"See the way he's incredibly focussed but relaxed at the same time?"

Lee saw. She attempted life through Bonnie's eyes. Alice and Will were studying the drummer as well. These three new people were doing something for her, this project of looking at a drummer. She felt a rise of affection as she imagined what the three of them saw: his eyes glazed, his hands rising up to a certain height and then falling back down as though they were attached to wires, someone who had a mission and who didn't care who knew it.

"He looks like he's in a trance."

"No, he's just perfected it."

She wanted them to see it. The pureness of it.

"Perfected what?"

"The art of playing."

Bonnie dug in her pocket for change.

*

My family

Family is who you live with. I live with Mum and Bonie and Alice. Alice is my sister. Mum is tall, Bonie is short. She plays drums in a band. Jacb plays giutar guitar. They are working on a record. Mum works in a library where men sleep. Mum is working on the gale. We have spagehtti sometimes, I don't like spagehtti. I can spell music Bonie taught me.

*